D1601503

Forever Watching You

M. A. COMLEY

OTHER BOOKS BY
NEW YORK TIMES BEST SELLING AUTHOR
M. A. COMLEY

Cruel Justice

Impeding Justice

Final Justice

Foul Justice

Guaranteed Justice

Ultimate Justice

Virtual Justice

Hostile Justice

Tortured Justice

Rough Justice (coming Jan 2015)

Blind Justice (A Justice novella)

Evil In Disguise (Based on true events)

Forever Watching You (#1 D I Miranda Carr Thrillers)

Torn Apart (Hero Series #1)

End Result (Hero Series #2)

Sole Intention (Intention Series #1)

Grave Intention (Intention Series #2)

It's A Dog's Life (A Lorne Simpkins short story)

ACKNOWLEDGMENTS

As always love and best wishes to my wonderful Mum for the role she plays in my career. Special thanks to my superb editor Stefanie, and my wonderful cover artist Karri. Thanks also to Joseph my amazing proof reader.

Licence Notes.

FOREVER WATCHING YOU

Prologue

After replacing the phone on the side table in the hallway, Anneka Morton said farewell to the world, for an hour or so anyway. The multi-millionairess intended to relax in a bubble bath, making the most of her husband's absence. The stiffness in her neck told her that she'd been burning the candle at both ends lately and for all the wrong reasons. If the long hours had involved champagne soirées, her complaints would have been more like dulled murmurings. However, the extra hours added to her already-hectic week were due to the pre-launch of a new product.

Owning a mega-successful cosmetics business had its ups and downs. *Don't all businesses?* She hoped the instructions she'd just given her personal assistant would clear her evening, if only for a few hours. *Give me that at least, please?* At age thirty-seven, she worked longer hours than most people her age did, but she was lost without the adrenaline rush that filled her when the pressure mounted. And no rush was bigger than the ones she had when a new product found its way out of her head and onto the marketplace.

Enough. Switch off and relax, she told herself, stepping into her round Jacuzzi tub filled with lavender-scented bubbles. Settling into the water, she reached for her glass of champagne then took a few sips. "This is the life. Maybe one of these days I'll be able to put my feet up and trust someone else to run the business for me." She closed her eyes and imagined the devastation that could bring— she'd spent a lifetime building her brand name. *Do I really have the courage to let a stranger get their mucky paws on it?* The scare stories she'd heard at parties had been plenty to warn her of the pitfalls of such decisions. The question was: did she really have the staying power? The strength of will and inclination to continue to grow her business? More to the point, would her husband, Bradley, put up with the neglect she showed him? She suspected his eye might start to wander. After all, men adored being the centre of a woman's affection.

As the stress seeped away from her body, she closed her eyes and smiled as the image of her handsome husband filled her mind. Envisioning herself in his strong arms sent a thrill scampering along her spine. The last five years had been awesome and totally unexpected, an adrenaline-filled adventure all the way. From the moment they had laid eyes on each other on that plane—his plane— her heart had never recovered. He'd become part of her, under her skin and in every crevice of her soul. At the time, Brad had just launched a corporate travel business for executives. The first time she had ever used such a company to travel across Europe, visiting the many experts she employed, he had piloted the plane himself. Maybe it was his captain's uniform that had initially set her heart fluttering. Whatever had caused her emotions to rocket into the stratosphere during that initial meeting, to this day they were inseparable, mostly.

Things had drastically changed lately, though, because of the failure of Brad's business. After refusing to give up on his dream, he was out there day and night, trying to find an investor for his new enterprise. *If only the economy would recover enough to allow such extravagances as executive travel for company board members...* She prayed for that day to come, for both their sakes.

Stop it! You're supposed to be relaxing. Listening to the Luther Vandross song emanating from the speaker system she and Brad had installed the previous month, Anneka watched the bubbles popping in her glass.

* * *

The two of them had no need to break in—they had a key to the house. And the stupid woman had forgotten to lock the gates again.

"We should be quiet from here. I can hear the music playing upstairs. She'll be up there, probably soaking in the bath."

The two masked figures, dressed from head-to-toe in black, ascended the stairs and followed the sound of the music along the thick-carpeted hallway.

They halted outside the master bedroom.

"We'll surprise her. Make sure your gloves are pulled on tight. The last thing we want is to leave any kind of prints." Bending down, the person in charge fiddled with the plastic bags covering his shoes, ensuring that the elastic was tight around his ankles. They had thought over the plan, thrashed out every trivial detail. The police would have a devil of a job finding and convicting them.

"Nice house," the second intruder whispered.

"Quiet, you'll give the game away. Are you ready?"

"Yes. Let's get this over with."

He gave the thumbs-up signal, and his accomplice returned the gesture.

"Go," he whispered and stormed into the room.

The woman screamed, dropped her glass, and tried to reach for a towel the second she saw them.

"Keep quiet, and you won't get hurt," the first intruder's deep voice boomed above the sound of the music.

"Please, please, don't hurt me. I'll give you anything you want. I have money, jewellery—anything and everything I have could be yours. Just don't hurt me, I beg you."

"Shut up."

The woman shrank back and gathered the bubbles to hide her naked flesh.

"Get out." The intruder picked up a luxurious white towelling robe and threw it at the woman. The robe landed in the water, but the woman quickly scooped it out. She stood up carefully, holding the robe in front of her. She turned sideways to save part of her modesty, slipped into the garment, and started to step out of the bath. But she suddenly lost her footing and fell into the water, banging her head on the tap in the middle of the bath as she went down.

For an instant, the two intruders stared at the still body covered by the bubbles, not really knowing what to do next. Realising they should do something to save the woman, they both rushed forward. Each of them grabbed a limp arm, and together, they lifted the woman, weighted down by the soaking-wet robe, out of the tub.

Panic filled their next few decisions.

"Is she dead?" the second intruder asked.

"No, I don't think so. Shit! What am I? A bloody doctor?"

"Don't snap at me. Do something!"

The intruder felt for a pulse on the woman's elegant, swanlike neck. "Nothing. Shit! What the fuck do we do now?"

"Get rid of the body."

"What? Why would we even contemplate doing that?"

The second intruder shrugged. "I don't know. You fucking come up with a solution then."

Both of them stood and anxiously began pacing the room. Their gazes drifted down to the woman's lifeless body every now and again. Finally, the leader formulated another plausible plan. But first, he needed two items from downstairs. "I'll be right back."

He raced to the kitchen and removed one of the knives from the wooden knife block. Then he ran back into the hallway and rolled up the black and white rug that covered the marble floor.

He dragged the heavy rug back up the stairs, wondering if he shouldn't have brought the body down instead. However, the woman's bleeding head would leave a trail throughout the house if they moved her first. This way, all the blood would remain inside the rug and in the bathroom. That should confuse the police. He dug deep and summoned up the extra muscle power to hoist the cumbersome carpet through the bedroom and eventually into the bathroom.

"What the heck?"

"Okay, here's what I'm thinking. We'll dump the body in the river. The light is fading, so no one will see us. We'll wrap her up in the rug first and throw her in the boot of the car."

"Okay, makes sense. I suggest doing the same thing. Where does the knife come into it?"

"We need to make sure she's dead before we dump the body, idiot!"

"You felt her pulse. Did you find one? No. Therefore, the bitch is dead. And don't call me an idiot, you friggin' prick!"

"There's no use arguing the toss around here. We should get this sorted and fuck off. The longer we stick around, the more chance there is of us being discovered here." He bent over the body and aimed the knife at the woman's chest. Pulling back the robe to expose her perfectly round breasts, he angled the knife over where he guessed the woman's heart was. Eyes clenched shut, he forced the point of the blade into the woman's flesh. For added certainty, he leaned over the knife and pushed it in farther. He felt the blade hit a bone before it continued its journey.

"Jesus! Talk about overkill. Was that bloody necessary?" the second intruder made the sign of a cross and stared at the dark-red blood flowing swiftly from the wound as the first intruder withdrew the knife.

"Yes, it was. Stop fucking questioning everything I do." He unrolled the rug, instructed his associate to help him move the body, and threw the knife in alongside the corpse. Then they rolled up the carpet again.

"How the hell are we going to get it down the stairs? She's not fat, but the weight of the body and the rug combined isn't going to be easy to shift."

"I've thought of that—another reason I enlisted the aid of the rug, in fact. We'll slide it down. It'll be easier to control, you'll see. Trust me. I know what to do."

"Trust you! Well, that's a laugh. If I had listened to my inner voice, I wouldn't be involved in this shit in the first place, but your powers of persuasion got me into this shitty mess. I'll regret that decision until the day I die."

"All right, wind your neck in. Less self-pity and more action. Once this is finished, we can go our separate ways if that's what you want. I ain't fucking bothered."

Anneka Morton looked down at her body in horror, a cold chill settling around her trembling shoulders. "What are they doing? Why can't I get up?"

It hadn't dawned on her that her life had just ended.

"Why are they rolling me in a rug? "Hey, you! That rug cost over five thousand pounds. You can't treat it like that—or me, for that matter! Stop!"

She watched the two masked people heave the rug wrapping her body through her beautiful bedroom, then they halted at the top of the stairs. "What are they doing now?"

The slightly smaller person placed one end of the rug at the top of the stairs and ran around to where the second person was standing.

"Ease it down gently. Try and hold the seam closed. If that comes open, we've had it," the taller one instructed.

"Won't the body come out? Maybe I should be in front of it, making sure it goes down slowly and intact."

"That makes sense. Go on then, what are you waiting for?"

The smaller one ran down a few treads and gripped the rug.

Anneka winced as she observed the rough way they were handling her rug—and her. She wanted to cry out in pain every time her body bounced down another step. The pair struggled to half-lift and half-drag her body to the double oak doors at the front of the house and out into the car, which was too dark for her to see what make or model it was. Unable to move, she felt glued to the spot. *With fear?* Three doors slammed, and the car drove off, kicking up the gravel in its haste.

She paced the hallway for hours. Two hours later, a tired and dishevelled Brad came through the front door.

"Oh, boy, am I glad you're home," Anneka said. She ran towards him, but he acted as if he couldn't see her. Confused, she sat on the bottom step of the sweeping staircase and watched her husband. When he passed her and went upstairs, she followed him into the bedroom, where he collapsed on the bed and promptly fell asleep.

"My poor, love, you must be exhausted from your trip. Aren't you surprised I'm not around? Go in the bathroom. Quickly, see what those terrible people did to me." She tried to shove her husband off the bed, but her hands disappeared into his body. Shocked, Anneka sat on the bed and sobbed for hours as the reality of the situation resolved in her mind, while her husband lay sleeping softly beside her, oblivious to what had occurred within the house during the past few hours.

The next morning, Brad woke with a start and shot off the bed. He ran into the bathroom and stopped dead in the doorway. His trembling hand swept over his face. Gulping at the sight of the blood on the bathroom floor, he bolted back into the bedroom and picked up the phone.

"Police, please… my wife is missing, and there's blood in my house."

He gave the woman his address and hung up. "Anneka, my love!" Tears streamed down his colourless cheeks. He looked stunned beyond words.

"I'm here, Brad. I'll always be here, sweetheart. Be brave, my love. I'll be forever watching you."

CHAPTER ONE

"Okay, guys, let's stop congratulating each other and get on with solving the next case," Detective Inspector Miranda Carr told her team jovially. She walked into her office and closed the door. Letting out a relieved sigh, she dropped into her chair. The love of her life, otherwise known as her fiancé, beamed at her from the framed picture she'd taken on holiday in Malta the previous year. Alan Rogers was her constant companion in coloured ink in the office and in the flesh at home. Miranda couldn't wait until they turned their cohabitation status into marriage. With the wedding only a month away, she still had tons, no exaggeration, left to do.

Alan was doing his best to help with organising the big day, but Miranda was such a control freak that she checked and double-checked every single detail to the point of driving him nuts. Numerous times, she had reprimanded herself, and she tried constantly to resist the temptation, only to fail miserably every time. Each day seemed to bring an extra problem, leaving her wondering why they hadn't simply jumped in the damn car and hiked it up to Gretna Green to tie the knot. She cringed, imagining the screaming fit both their mothers would have if that scenario materialised. Miranda and Alan's lives wouldn't be worth living, for one thing.

A knock on the door disrupted her daydream. She picked up some paperwork, wanting to give her visitor the impression that she was super busy. Her partner, Detective Sergeant Johnny Tomlin, poked his head around the door. "Do you have a spare few minutes for a chat?"

Her brow creased, and she beckoned him in. "Any time, you know that. You look worried. What's up?"

"Nothing major. I just need a bit of advice. It's kind of personal."

Miranda sat back in her chair and crossed her arms. "Sounds ominous. Go on."

To Miranda's trained eye, Johnny seemed a little agitated. He shuffled uncomfortably in his seat until he finally formed his sentence. "I've got problems."

Miranda smiled, encouraging him to continue, but remained silent.

"You know the group of boys I've been kind of mentoring down at the community centre?"

"Yes. Come on, Johnny, out with it."

"Well, two of them got arrested yesterday."

"Oh no, really? For what?"

He rubbed a hand over the right side of his face. "Shoplifting."

"What? Why are you so glum about this? Don't all kids chance their arm now and again at shoplifting sweets?" She remembered how tempted she had been during her rebellious teens.

"Sweets! I bloody wish. They got caught nicking two bottles of whiskey."

"Jeez, that isn't good. Did they tell you why?"

"I questioned them until I was blue in the face. They finally broke down and told me it was some kind of dare given to them by an older boy. Not one of mine, I hasten to add."

"So they got arrested, and what? Were they let off with a caution, as it's their first offence?"

"Nope. The thing is, these two boys have been in bother with the law for a while now. I thought I was making some headway with them. Obviously, I was wrong about that."

"Don't be too hard on yourself, Johnny. Kids are prone to veering off in all sorts of directions even under the most disciplined of parents. You're doing a great job down at the centre. What does Jeff say about the incident?"

"He's as frustrated as me. We've been putting extra effort into spending more time with the two boys. To have them shit on us like this is utterly exasperating."

"Hey, stick with it, mate. If you give up on these kids, then what hope is there for them?"

"You don't realise what a bloody strain it is to keep them straight. Christ, if I'd behaved the way they do at that age, my dad would have thrashed the life out of me with my plimsoll."

Miranda chuckled. "Gosh, now there's a word I haven't heard in a long time. I do believe you're showing your age."

"What? Twenty-eight? Give it a rest, boss."

Another knock sounded on the office door. "Enter," Miranda called out.

DC Craig Fulford joined them. "We've just had a strange call, ma'am. Thought you might like to check it out yourself."

Miranda raised an enquiring eyebrow and glanced down at her messy desk, laden with post and case files. "And you reckon that because you don't think I've got anything better to do? Or because I'm the only one on this team capable of solving a major crime? Which is it, Craig?"

"Umm... neither. I mean, I just thought you should know, ma'am," the young man stuttered.

When his cheeks deepened in colour, Miranda grimaced, embarrassed about teasing the DC. She held out her hand. "Do you have the address for me?"

Fulford tutted and disappeared for a second or two. He returned and passed her a piece of paper. "Sorry, ma'am. It's one of the very posh houses in Mill Hill. Uphill Road, actually."

"What's the crime, Craig?"

"The gentleman of the house states that his wife is missing and there's a large pool of blood in the bathroom."

"That's strange. And he has no idea where she could be?"

Craig shrugged, and his mouth turned down at the sides. "He said she's nowhere to be seen, ma'am."

Miranda glanced at her partner and smiled. "Can we discuss your issue on the way?"

Johnny dismissed the notion with a wave of his hand. "No need. My problem will sort itself out in the next few days. Do you want to set off now?"

"Might as well. There's nothing urgent here, from what I can tell. The fresh air will do us both some good."

In the car, Miranda revisited the topic that was worrying her partner. "So, what are you going to do about the boys? Keep a closer eye on them?"

"That would be a full-time job in itself. Jeff intends to separate the boys while they're at the centre, but that won't help when they aren't under either his supervision or mine."

"Are these boys from foster homes? I know we shouldn't use that as an excuse, of course."

"Yes, most of the boys down there are from foster homes. All they need is a good male role model in their lives, and I'm not talking about pop stars or footie stars, either. Most of those are on bloody drugs, from what I can tell."

Miranda quickly looked at him then back at the busy road ahead. "What? Footballers on drugs?"

"No. The footballers are just spoilt tossers. Sorry, I was referring to most of the pop stars out there today. What kind of role models are they to these young kids?"

"I understand. It must be frustrating for both you and the foster parents. That can't be an easy load on anyone, especially if, like you, they have full-time careers."

"It's definitely becoming more of a struggle. We'll get there, though. What do you think about the case?"

"I can't even begin to hazard a guess. Let's go into the house with a clear head and take it from there, yes?"

"Okay with me. How are the wedding plans progressing?"

"Umm… let's avoid that subject, too, eh?"

"That bad! Not sure why you're even considering taking the plunge anyway. Live in sin—it's the norm, isn't it?"

"Alan and I would have no qualms continuing to do that, but our parents are making our lives hell. They've started badgering us for grandchildren."

"No way! Does that mean you'll be retiring from the force?"

Miranda chortled. "Why? Would you be interested in the vacancy?"

"Oh no, I didn't mean that. I could never fill your shoes. No one could."

"I only wear size four, so you'd have a job. No, this is just our way of softening the blow for when we tell our parents that neither of us *want* children of our own."

"Don't envy you that job. Do they have any idea you feel that way? All parents crave to be grandparents eventually."

Miranda shook her head and glanced sideways. "Nope. It's all good fun, isn't it? What about you and Francis? You've been dating for longer than Alan and me, haven't you?"

"No way, José! I think people are crazy even to consider tying the knot nowadays. Have you read the divorce statistics lately? Nope, I don't intend ever being classed as a hen-pecked husband. I enjoy my freedom too much."

Miranda ignored the jibe about the divorce statistics and joked, "You mean you enjoy your shameless flirting with anything in a skirt and wearing a low top."

"Moi? It's all harmless fun. Girls shouldn't flaunt their wares if they don't want us guys to letch over them."

"I'm not your mother, matey. You don't have to try and cover my eyes with wool or justify your scandalous behaviour to me."

"Take the next right," Johnny said, pointing ahead.

"Thanks, I've got sat nav, remember? And stop bloody changing the subject like that."

After a few more turnings, Johnny pointed at a large pair of gates set in a high white-walled entranceway. Miranda whistled. "Holy crap! What's the betting this place has an indoor pool and a home cinema sitting in the cellar?"

"I think that's a given. Let's see if we can get in." He pressed a button on the intercom and leaned out of the window to announce them. The intercom buzzed, and the gates opened slowly to reveal a stunning home of brick and glass tucked behind a sweeping lawn ablaze with orange and red flowers. "Wow, Mum and Dad would go bananas over a garden like this."

"How's their garden centre doing now?"

"They're slowly rebuilding after the fire. The insurance company took an eternity to sort a payment out. They are just getting to grips with restocking and restaffing the place. Thanks for asking."

"Did our lot ever catch the culprits who struck the match?"

"Not yet. I'm just glad Dad had chosen to work late that night and was there to call the brigade quickly. Not that it prevented the fire from spreading."

"It could have been far worse. Big relief all round, I should imagine."

Miranda switched off the engine, and they both climbed out of the car. "This is truly amazing—or 'amazeballs,' as the kids of today would say."

"There has to be a lot of money invested within these walls."

Miranda agreed. When she rang the bell, she could tell how grand the house was by the number of times the chime echoed around the interior.

Seconds later, a man dressed in a black suit and evening shirt opened the front door, sporting stubble on his wrinkle-free face.

"Mr. Lawrence? I'm DI Miranda Carr, and this is my partner, DS Johnny Tomlin. All right if we come in?"

The shell-shocked man stepped aside to let them into the huge marble-and-white hallway. "Have you found her?"

"Your wife?" The man nodded. "Not yet. Is there somewhere we can have a chat?"

"Don't you want to see where it happened? To get the ball rolling in your investigation?"

"If that's what you would like, Mr. Lawrence. We can check it out for ourselves if you'd rather stay downstairs."

"No, I'll show you." He trudged up the staircase in front of the two detectives and led them into the bathroom; the scene of the crime.

Miranda shook her head. By the amount of blood pooling on the chequered black-and-white bathroom tiles, she saw no point even considering the man's wife was still alive. No one could survive losing that amount of blood. Seeing her partner's grim expression told her he knew that they'd be looking for a corpse, too.

"Call SOCO," Miranda instructed Johnny. He left the room, and she could hear him speaking on his mobile in the main bedroom while she began asking Mr. Lawrence a few simple questions, fearing that the man might crumble if she started with the most awkward questions first. "Have you walked any further into the room at all?"

"No. I saw the blood and backed out immediately to ring you... er... the police."

"And this is the only room that contains traces of any blood?"

"Yes. Everywhere else is spotless, just the way it was when I left the house."

"Can you go through what happened, Mr. Lawrence?"

"I've been away. I came back to find the house empty. I collapsed on the bed, fully clothed. I was that exhausted, as you can see, Inspector." He ran a hand through his curls and messed them up even more.

"Away? For what reason?"

"Business, as in trying to summon up some through my contacts."

"I see." Miranda raised an eyebrow. "Can you take down some notes, Sergeant?" she ordered her partner when he returned.

Johnny withdrew his notebook from his jacket pocket and flipped over a couple of pages, prepared to jot down Mr. Lawrence's replies as Miranda asked the questions.

"How long have you been away, Mr. Lawrence?" Miranda asked.

"Two days."

"Can you tell us where?"

"Abroad, in Portugal."

"Okay, was your wife expecting you to return yesterday?"

"No. I thought I would surprise her. That's why I wasn't overly concerned when she wasn't here. I presumed she had gone out to dinner with friends or something." He sat down heavily on the end of the bed, rested his elbows on his knees, and buried his head in his hands. "Why? Why would someone do this to my wife?"

"That's what I intend to find out, Mr. Lawrence. I'm going to have to ask you for a list of her friends and family members so we can begin our investigation. While you're at it, you might also consider telling us about any people who might have some form of vendetta, either against you or your wife."

He glanced up at Miranda and frowned. "Good Lord, do you realise what you're saying?"

"What do you mean, Mr. Lawrence?"

The man sighed, forcing a large breath of air from his lungs. "My wife is an international businesswoman with a product—or I should say 'range of products'—that the most influential people in the cosmetic industry are envious of. That kind of notoriety comes with more negatives than positives, I can assure you."

"Well, I can certainly understand that, but we'll still need to have a full list of names, the sooner the better."

He covered his eyes and shook his head. "All I want is my wife back. If you won't get out there and look for her, then *I* will." He launched himself off the bed, and Miranda quickly stood aside as he raced her way. He brushed past her and hurried out of the room.

"Do you want me to go after him?" Johnny asked.

"No. Let him blow off steam by himself for a moment or two. Shit! Our priority has to be to find this woman. Ring the station and organise a press conference ASAP, would you?" She lowered her voice to say the final part. "That's the best start we can make without a body."

"Do you think we should call a member of his family to come and sit with him? He looks distraught. Is there a chance he might contemplate doing something silly?"

"Good thinking. Let's see if anyone lives close by."

The two detectives walked back down the grand staircase to find the man sitting at the granite island in the enormous kitchen.

"Mr. Lawrence, we think you should have someone here with you. A family member or friend, perhaps," Miranda said.

"No! I don't need any of them. I just want Anneka back." He flew off the barstool, flung open the patio door, and bolted into the rear garden.

"Touchy, ain't he?" Johnny commented.

"How would you react if Francis went missing? Let's give him a bit of slack for a few days, eh?"

"I suppose you're right. I'll ring the station."

Miranda nodded and cast her eye around the room. The whole room was white, except for the black granite tops. She spotted the stark combination as a theme running throughout the house. She searched a few of the cupboards, looking for a cup or mug to make the man a coffee, but couldn't find any. Then she realised there wasn't even a kettle in sight. *How odd.*

Just then, Mr. Lawrence returned to the room. She smiled and held her arms out to the side. "I was trying to make you a coffee. You do drink coffee in this house, don't you?"

He moved to the floor-to-ceiling cupboards and pulled two mugs from one of the drawer units. Then he filled the mugs with instant coffee granules and sugar from the contents of another drawer. Miranda was puzzled by what the man did next. Taking the mugs, he placed them under the tap on the sink set into the island. She was just about to tell him that he'd made a mistake when she noticed steam rising from the cup.

"There you go, Inspector."

"Wow, is that a magic tap?"

"No. Not really. I think they've been around for a while. Anneka hated—I mean, hates clutter on the sides, so we invested in a tap that delivers boiling hot water 'on tap,' if you will."

"Amazing. Drink up. Coffee ails all problems, so I'm told."

"It might do, the question is, will it help bring my wife back?" He sat down at the long kitchen table and twisted his mug on the glass coaster.

Miranda joined him, uncertain what to say next. Time was rapidly getting away from them, and it was urgent they get things moving. Nonetheless, she didn't want to seem callous. Sometimes an inspector, or any serving officer, needed to push his or her compassionate side to the fore to deal with the relative's grief.

Johnny disturbed the awkward silence when he entered the kitchen a few minutes later. "Conference booked for four this afternoon, boss."

"Excellent. That'll be our chance to ask the public for help to try and find your wife, Mr. Lawrence."

"I hope it goes well for you," the man replied, seeming distracted.

The two detectives glanced at each other and shrugged. "Just so it's clear—we want you to attend the conference. A plea from you will certainly help."

He sat back in his chair, the rising panic evident. "I can't. Not on national TV."

Miranda placed her hand on top of his, noting how much it was shaking. "I understand how hard all of this must be for you, but it would work in Anneka's favour for you to attend. You needn't speak. I can do all the talking for you, so there's no problem in that respect. Even down to the plea, you could write out what you wanted to say. I'd be happy to relay that message on your behalf."

"Now? We really have to do this now? All I want is the safe return of my wife. Won't we be wasting time? Shouldn't you be out there, searching for her?"

"I understand your frustration, Mr. Lawrence. Sorry, do you mind if I call you Brad?"

"Go ahead. It's my name," he replied abruptly, then offered a brief smile as an apology for his dubious attitude.

"Brad, in these types of cases, it's important that we get as much background information as we can. Otherwise, if we go hell for leather, searching here, there, and everywhere, we're sure to be pulled in the wrong direction. That's sod's law and a copper's worst enemy, apart from the villains." She tried the light-hearted approach to see if the man would open up more.

"If you say so. Do you have a pad and pen?"

Johnny withdrew his notebook, but Miranda shook her head. "We need something better than that." She handed her partner the keys to the car. "My briefcase is in the boot. I think there's a shorthand notebook inside."

"Okay." Johnny started to walk out of the kitchen as crunching gravel in the driveway alerted them to a vehicle arriving.

"That's probably SOCO. Let them in, will you, Johnny?" After her partner had left the room, Miranda asked Brad, "Off the top of your head, do you think we should start looking in a certain direction first? Anyone with a recent grudge perhaps?"

"Anneka is just about to launch a new skin-care range. It's taken her two years of travelling back and forth to see the supplies abroad and to arrange everything. In that time, Inspector, my wife has probably crushed many toes and pissed off several people to get to this point. The launch is set to take place in a few days. Crap, I'll have to cancel everything now—the venue, the press party, the launch party itself. Jesus, when am I going to get the chance to help look for Anneka with all that shit to do?"

"Leave the search for us to carry out, Brad. One question, if I may? Why do you need to cancel everything if it's all in place ready to go anyway?"

"What? Are you crazy? I know very little about the business. I couldn't carry on with a launch. Not only that, what about the fact that she's missing? Can you imagine the furore that would evolve from that situation? People would probably draw straws to lynch me."

"Okay, I understand there are issues. Nevertheless, would you really want to see your wife's hard work over the last few years go to waste like that? What will Anneka say if we find her and she discovers you called off the launch at the very last minute? There must be exorbitant cost implications to consider in all of this, too. Surely, your wife has staff who could deal with the launch for you? If that's what you're concerned about?"

"She has. Oh, crap, I don't know. Yes, her competitors would rub their hands together if I called years of dedicated work off with the click of my fingers, but I say again, how will I be perceived by the rest of the world? 'Oh, there he is. The wife's missing, dead for all we know, but he's still out there, intent on raking the money in.' I can hear them saying it now."

Miranda shook her head. She wouldn't like that dilemma thrown at her door, for sure. "Okay, here's what I want to suggest. Let's concentrate on working out your speech for the conference, create the lists of possible suspects, and then consider what to do about the business, specifically the launch. If you give me the name of your wife's assistant, I can give her a ring to see how advanced things are and ask the question if she feels capable of taking care of things from here."

Brad thought her suggestion over for several seconds, his ears and eyes trained on the people filtering through the hallway and making their way upstairs to the crime scene.

"Her assistant is called Jess. Jessica Tomasson. I'll get you her number."

He left the table, giving Miranda the impression that she'd managed to talk him out of a hasty decision. When he returned, he placed a piece of paper with a number written on it in front of her.

"Let me deal with this while you make a start on the list of suspects. I want names, dates of any other instances that you think I should be aware of, things like that. Have you informed Anneka's parents yet?"

His fist thumped the side of his head. "Shit, it completely slipped my mind. They'll be devastated. They're travelling around South Devon right now."

"Do they have a mobile?"

"Yes, but I can't ring them." He looked horrified.

"Is there some reason why not?" Miranda raised a questioning eyebrow.

"How can I tell them that sort of news? That their daughter is missing and presumed dead. I just can't."

"That's the thing—we don't know if Anneka is dead or not. So just tell them that she's missing at present. The call would be better coming from someone they know instead of me."

He inhaled and exhaled a few deep breaths as he thought. Finally, he flung his hands up in the air and crossed the room to pick up the house phone. He punched in a number he'd looked up from a book lying beside the phone.

"Hello, Sheila. How's the holiday going?" Brad asked his mother-in-law.

Miranda watched the man fidget, avoiding eye contact with her during his brief conversation. She understood how awkward he must feel sharing such dreadful news with his in-laws.

"The thing is, Sheila, and the reason behind my call is that, well… Anneka has gone missing."

Miranda could imagine the frantic response on the other end of the line.

"Now, Sheila, there's no point you coming back until we have more news. Stay where you are, and I'll keep you informed." He swiftly held the phone away from his ear then spoke into it again,

"Sheila, are you still there?" Replacing the phone in its holder, Brad returned to stand in front of Miranda.

"I take it that didn't go down too well?"

"No. She and her husband are driving back immediately. To be honest, that's the last thing I need right now."

"The support is what you need, Brad."

"Yeah, but that support is going to come with a price. It always does with Sheila and James. I've never been good enough for their daughter. Our relationship has been even more strained since the collapse of my own business. I think they see me as some kind of gold digger now, living off their daughter." He sank into the chair, exhausted by the revelation.

"I see. I'm sorry to hear that. I would have made the call myself if I'd been aware of the situation between all of you. In times such as this, families tend to pull together in order to find the victim."

He turned to look at her and snorted. "You think? I get the impression it's going to make things a thousand times worse. They're tough people. It's hard to win over their affections. Still, that's my problem, not yours."

"Does Anneka get on with her parents?"

"Yes, very well. It's only me they have a problem with. What happens next?"

"Let's work on what you want to say or for me to say at the conference, unless you'd rather your in-laws do all the talking in front of the camera? They should be back from Devon by then, shouldn't they?"

"That's an idea. Sheila loves to hear the sound of her own voice. I'm sorry, that was uncalled for. It's just that I've had so many problems with these people in the past."

"Let's forget about them for now. If they leave within the next half an hour, they should be back here for what, one or two?"

"Yep, I guess."

Miranda jotted down a few key points she thought either of them should mention during the conference. For the time being, Brad remained undecided about making the public plea himself. Maybe he would summon up the inner strength once his feelings of uselessness had dissipated. Miranda felt if he did speak out, it might show his in-laws how much he cared about their daughter.

"Okay, I'll leave you to get on with that list of suspects, if you will? I'll just go upstairs and see how things are progressing with the Scenes of Crimes officers."

"All right, I'll try and think of everyone we've fallen out with. I'm warning you, though, it's going to be an extensive list."

Miranda nodded and left the room. *Crap! I hope it's not too long.*

CHAPTER TWO

"Anything come to light so far, boys?" Miranda asked, poking her head into the en suite bathroom.

The younger of the two suited-and-booted men crouching down, taking samples of the blood from the tiled floor, replied, "Looking at the scene, the full tub, the blood in the water and on the tap, et cetera, I reckon the victim was actually inside the tub initially. However, looking at the amount of water outside the tub, I don't think she put up any kind of struggle."

"Meaning, you don't think that she was drowned by someone?"

"Yep, although I could be wrong of course. If someone is in the process of being drowned, they tend to thrash about, trying to ward off their attacker."

"Unless the victim is unconscious? What's with the blood on the tap?" Miranda asked.

The man shrugged. "Pure speculation at this point, perhaps whoever attacked her bashed her head against the tap first as a means of knocking her out."

"So, she might have been drowned after all," Miranda suggested.

"Every possibility. We'll keep searching for clues for now."

She pulled her partner away from the doorway. "I think this is going to turn out to be a very complex and, at times, frustrating case."

"Aren't they all to begin with? How's the husband holding up? Are you looking at him as a possible suspect yet?" Johnny asked.

"I'm still undecided about that. I'd like to keep him onside until after the conference. At the moment, he seems a little more relaxed. Not sure how long that will last, though."

"How come?"

"He had to call the in-laws, and he doesn't actually get on too well with them. They're on their way back from holiday right now. I'm still working on him making the appeal himself. Only time will tell on that one. I hope he does—I hate it when the victim's family is sitting alongside me, too distraught to talk to the camera."

"Yeah, we tend to get more results when the families speak out rather than when you do all the talking. Maybe people hate your voice or something."

Miranda swiped his arm. "Have I told you lately how good you are for my self-esteem?"

Johnny sniggered. "You know I mean that in a kind and caring way. So, what's next?"

"Hmm… I'm not so sure with you sometimes. Well, Brad is getting together a list of possible suspects for us, which by the sounds of it, could be quite lengthy. Next stop will be to start interviewing all those on the list. I have an inkling that a lot of them will be abroad, so I'll have to get in touch with our Interpol friends, see if they can offer some assistance." She leaned in and whispered, "Between you and me, I hope they put up the barriers and refuse. I could do with a break in a hot climate somewhere."

Her partner tutted. "Yeah, like that's going to happen. Oh, wait a minute—I forgot how close you are to the chief. She'll do anything to keep you happy and part of her team."

Miranda shut her eyes and tipped her chin into the air. "It doesn't suit you to be envious, Johnny."

He laughed. "Yeah, right. You know me, hate sucking up to my superiors."

"I had noticed."

The pair laughed and left the SOCO team to get on with their work. On the way back downstairs, Miranda checked each step of the staircase thoroughly, looking for signs of blood. "She or they must have come down this way."

"Unless the abductor or intruder dumped her body out of the upstairs window to avoid leaving possible DNA clues throughout the house. You know how crafty these people are getting, thanks to all these TV forensic shows."

"You could have a point there." She ran back up the stairs and through the master bedroom. "There's no visible sign of blood or anything on the staircase. My partner came up with the idea that Anneka's body might have been thrown out the window. Can you guys check for any signs of that please? After you've finished in here, of course."

"Sure."

She retraced her steps once again and joined her partner at the bottom of the staircase. Pondering their next move, she looked around the hallway. "Isn't this place amazing? I bet they employed the likes of an interior designer to kit this out. They must have. Everything matches perfectly. Nothing's garish or looks out of place." She crossed the hallway and stared at the marble floor. "Hey, what's this?" She crouched to take a closer look. "It's dust. Or dirt, more like."

"But this place is immaculate. Not a speck of dust on any of the furniture or skirtings, from what I can see from here."

"Precisely!" Miranda waited for Johnny to get her drift. "So? What do you think was here? Some kind of rug?" she asked.

Johnny frowned for a second, and he nodded. "Seems like that to me."

Miranda stood up and winked at her partner. "Come with me."

They found Brad in the lounge, still busy scribbling down names in the notebook.

"Sorry to interrupt, Brad," Miranda said. "We've just noticed something in the hallway. Do you mind coming with us?"

The man set aside the notebook and followed Miranda. "What? Don't tell me you've found more blood?"

"No. Can you tell me if anything's missing from your house?"

He glanced around. "Not that I can think of, Inspector. Truthfully, my wife is the one bothered by possessions, not me. You could say she's obsessed in that regard. What are you referring to?"

"Take a closer look. Focus on the floor, maybe."

Brad hit his forehead with the heel of his hand. "Of course, the bloody rug's gone. Maybe Anneka asked the cleaner to send it to the dry cleaners or something."

"Really? Don't carpet cleaners usually take care of that?"

"I don't know, Inspector. I can ring the cleaner if you like and ask."

Miranda smiled. "Give Johnny her number, and he'll chase it up. I'd like you to continue with your list. That's of greater importance right now." She dismissed the man and remained in the hallway with Johnny.

"We'll get the cleaner's number off him in a sec. Do you know in which way my line of thinking is going?" Miranda asked her partner.

"Not sure yet. Let me have it?"

"Maybe the intruder rolled Anneka's body up in the rug and took her out of the house that way."

Johnny's eyes narrowed as he thought. "I suppose it's possible. That would be quite a weight, I should imagine. Don't disturb the hubby anymore about the size of the rug. I'll ask the cleaner. The likelihood of it being a small rug is pretty minimal, though, given the size of the hallway. A small rug would look pathetic, even to mere mortals like us."

"I agree on everything you've raised and some."

"You do have the annoying habit of talking in riddles sometimes. Let's have it, boss."

"What if we're looking at *two* intruders?"

Johnny pointed his finger in the air then placed it on his lips as he pondered. "Now that's a good idea. You could be on to something. I'll ring the cleaner first then skirt around the house, see if I can find where they keep their surveillance equipment. Maybe looking at that will throw up some answers."

"Good idea. I'm really not liking the way this is panning out. I think we should section off the area as a crime scene. It's escalated from a possible to probable fatal crime scene, in my book anyway, which means that I'll have to tell Brad to leave his home. I can't see that going down too well."

"Shit happens. Until we find the wife's body or are contacted by the abductors—if that is what we're dealing with—I think you're making the right call."

Miranda straightened her shoulders and stepped back into the lounge again. "How are you doing?" she asked Brad.

"Almost there. I think."

"You're not going to like what I'm about to say. Unfortunately, I find myself having to follow procedures."

"Inspector? What are you getting at?"

"In light of the situation we're dealing with, I have to ask you to move out of the marital home, for the time being."

"What? What if Anneka comes back? Hey, wait a minute. Are you saying what I think you're saying… that you're presuming my wife is dead and not just missing?"

Miranda swallowed hard. "If the rug was still in place, we'd still be thinking your wife might be merely missing. However, considering its removal from the premises, we have to believe that it was used with only one aim in mind—to hide your wife's body."

Brad appeared to be dumbstruck momentarily, and his eyes misted with tears. When he finally found his voice again, he said, "Dear Lord, my poor, poor wife. Please tell me you won't give up the search for her?"

"I want to assure you, Brad, there is no fear of that. We will find her. We're going to need to section your master bedroom off, from all and sundry trampling over what could be evidence. Do you want to leave the list for a while and collect some things before that?"

He placed the pad on the sofa beside him, stood up, and left the room. His shoulders slumped and his feet heavy, he made his way upstairs.

Johnny came into the lounge seconds later as Miranda was consulting the list, running her finger down the many names to see if she recognised any of them—she didn't. "Jesus, this is going to take us a frigging eternity to plough through. Any news?"

"Great. Right, I rang the cleaner, and she confirmed that there is always a rug in the hall. Actually, it's a brand-new one, approximately two months old. And, no, it hasn't gone to the cleaners. She cleans all the rugs herself—well, her husband does that side of things for her. So, that means your assumption is probably spot on."

"Sometimes, just sometimes, I hate being right all the time. It really does become tedious."

Johnny shook his head. "Have you added conceitedness to your extensive list of wonderful attributes yet, boss?"

Her eyes fluttered shut and opened again. "I'm always happy to add another envious attribute to my bow, dearest partner. There's no need for you to wear your envy so openly like that. It's not becoming."

"Whatever. What's next on the agenda? Oh, hang on—I got distracted making the call and forgot to snoop around for the surveillance equipment."

"We'll do that together."

They left the lounge and opened all the doors to the rooms that lead off the central hallway until they discovered what they were after. "This looks promising. Any idea what this stuff is?"

Johnny bent down to see the equipment better. "Looks like a simple DVD setup to me. Nothing very taxing, from what I can tell. Hmm..."

"What? Go on, surprise me."

"Looks like the machine is switched off."

Miranda looked at the monitor, which displayed four camera angles located around the home's perimeter. "So, the cameras are working, yet the recording machine is off?"

"That's my take on things. It's not hard to see the place has surveillance cameras once you pull up outside. Maybe the intruders disabled it before they did anything else."

"I'm hearing what you're saying, but wouldn't they attack the cameras outside first? Spray them or something?" Miranda queried.

"Fair point. In that case, I'm inclined to think the intruders knew exactly where the equipment was to avoid it and disable it."

"Looks that way. Which will narrow the search of possible suspects considerably. Let's keep this between us for now. I'm going to ask Brad to go through the list he's made, ticking off all those who have visited the home."

Johnny followed Miranda into the hallway and closed the door behind him. Lowering his voice, he told her, "I'll get SOCO to dust the equipment for prints, just in case the intruders were sloppy."

"Wait until Brad is back down here before you do that, all right?"

Miranda heard someone coming down the stairs at that moment, and she started going over how the rest of the day should pan out. "I'd like to wait around here until Anneka's parents arrive. SOCO will likely be here all day anyway."

"Okay, what do you want me to do?" Johnny asked.

"I think you should hang around here for a while. Let me see Brad off the premises first and get back to you."

Brad dropped his small case at the base of the stairs. "I'm ready to go, Inspector."

"Where will you be staying? I'll need a contact number for you."

"We have an apartment overlooking the river, where we stay when we nip into the city to see a show or something. Chelsea Harbour. Here's the number."

"One last thing before you go. I think we have enough names on the list for now to be getting on with it. If you can think of anyone else, be sure to ring me. Can you do me a favour and quickly tick off any people who have visited your home?"

His frown appeared but quickly dispersed. "Sure, that'll be easy. There's not many. My wife has neither the time nor energy for holding regular dinner parties. She is quite private in that respect. If she wants to entertain, it's either at the apartment in Chelsea Harbour or at a restaurant, where she always foots the bill. I'll do that now."

After Brad walked into the lounge, Miranda turned to Johnny. "When he comes back with the list, I want you to go through it and make appointments for us to see the people."

"From tomorrow, right?"

Miranda nodded. "Yeah, we have too much on today. I know it will add to our workload after the appeal goes out. Nonetheless, it's an important part of the investigation. We'll get the rest of the team sifting through the calls from the appeal and tackle Brad's list ourselves tomorrow."

Brad breezed into the hallway and held out the list for Miranda to take. She glanced down and nodded. "Not too many at all. We'll contact them today and go from there. I appreciate your help in this matter, Brad. I'll be in touch soon. Don't forget to show up at the police station about half an hour before the conference starts."

"I won't. I'll be off now and get cleaned up. Good luck with your investigations in the meantime, Inspector."

Miranda watched the dejected man leave the house. "Get on with the list, Johnny, and I'll go check on how things are progressing upstairs. Oh, and ring the station to get a couple of uniforms out here to section off the area, will you?"

"Got it."

Miranda walked upstairs again, constantly keeping an eye out for clues. "Guys, how's it going?" she asked the two SOCO men.

"We're nearly done in here."

"Good. After you've dusted the windows—although I suspect that's going to prove a waste of time now—looks like we have a rug missing downstairs. I think the body was probably transported out of the house that way, given the lack of blood spots throughout the rest of the house. Anyway, I digress—we have a small room downstairs where the surveillance equipment is housed, and I'd like you to dust that for prints, too. Looks like the machine was possibly switched off by the intruder or intruders."

"You've got it. I've taken the victim's hairbrush off the dressing table. We'll match the DNA from the blood on the floor and the tap to that. You never know, she might have lashed out and hurt her assailant."

"Okay. It's looking more and more like we'll be searching for a corpse, doesn't it?" she asked, knowing what the SOCO guys' answer would be before she finished her statement.

"It looks that way, yes," one of the officers replied with a grave nod.

Anneka watched intently over everything that went on in her house that morning, with tears brimming in her eyes. *Do spirits of the dead really cry?* she asked herself over and over again. Her heart went out to her beloved husband, who had looked distraught from the moment he saw her blood on the bathroom floor. When the detective asked Brad to leave the house, Anneka wondered if it would be possible to transport herself from one location to another. Perhaps she would need to be dead a certain amount of time before God gave her such divine powers. She would love to comfort her husband at their Chelsea Harbour home, the home where they had shared wonderful evenings, holding each other on the balcony overlooking the Thames, looking up to count the twinkling stars, and even naming a few of the brighter ones.

Once or twice, she found herself questioning the decisions of the inspector in charge of the case. But in the end, she thought the woman would do well and bring her killers to justice soon. Anneka liked her. What was there not to like about a slim, pretty woman in her early thirties with blonde hair pulled into a tight ponytail? The detective had a certain air of superiority. Anneka could imagine the woman exploding and ripping into someone who didn't perform a task how she wanted it to be carried out. *A bit like me in that respect!*

The other detective, the man, seemed capable of doing a good job, under the woman's leadership, of course. All men performed better under a woman's guidance and ability to look outside the box, especially where clues were concerned. She wondered how many male detectives would have spotted the missing rug. The detective's skills boded well for the team finding her body quickly. At the moment, she felt frustrated that she seemed unable to leave the house. *Come on, let me leave and find myself or what's left of me!*

CHAPTER THREE

Miranda's stomach growled violently. "Damn, I wonder if there's a baker's nearby?"

"Do you want me to send one of the PCs out to get us some lunch? I'm starving, too." Johnny rubbed his own tummy.

"Why not?" She dug into her jacket pocket and pulled out a twenty-pound note. "That should cover it."

"You think?" Johnny raised an eyebrow. "You have looked around you today, haven't you? What are the odds on this area demanding twenty quid a roll?"

"Crap, then we'll have to go halves and continue to battle the hunger pangs during the rest of the day, won't we?"

"We'll see."

By the time the PC returned with their baguettes, Anneka's parents had arrived at the house, dashing Miranda's hopes of eating lunch in peace. She instructed Johnny to eat in the kitchen while she spoke to the parents in the lounge.

Miranda motioned for the couple to take a seat on the couch. They sat down and clung to each other's hands so tightly that their knuckles turned white. "I'm sorry I had to drag you back from your holiday, Mr. and Mrs. Morton."

"You didn't. Our son-in-law did," Mrs. Morton corrected.

"I know, I'm sorry. This is where the investigation stands so far. Apparently, Mr. Lawrence, Brad, returned home and fell into bed, exhausted—"

"Ha! That'll be the day with that one. Sorry, carry on, Inspector," Mrs. Morton said, her lip turned up in disgust for the man.

"Well, it wasn't until the next day that Brad discovered blood in the en suite of the master bedroom. We believe the blood belongs to your daughter, but we have yet to verify that."

Mrs. Morton gasped and shook her head. "I have a very bad feeling about this, Inspector. My daughter, our beautiful daughter, is a very successful woman about to embark on yet another multi-million-pound launch of a new product range."

"Yes, so her husband told me. He's also given me a list of possible suspects, work-related people who might have gone out of their way to interfere with the launch."

"I doubt any of her competitors would have either the balls or the gumption to do such a thing."

Miranda tilted her head. "What are you saying, Mrs. Morton? That we should be looking closer to home?"

"You can't say that, darling—it's not fair. Just because you don't like the man doesn't mean that he would harm Anneka. He's always showed nothing but love for her," Mr. Morton was quick to suggest.

"You know my feelings, James. There's always been something about the man that I've disliked. What was your impression of him, Inspector? Truthfully, I mean."

"Gosh, well, to be honest, he seemed very distraught by his wife's disappearance. Spent the morning on the verge of tears, actually. Has he done anything in the past to make you dislike him so much, Mrs. Morton?"

"Apart from breathe?"

Miranda frowned and dropped into the two-seater sofa opposite the couple, noting the warning look James Morton issued his wife.

"Now, that's enough, dear. Why don't we hold back on asking questions here, Inspector, until after we've found our daughter?"

"Now ordinarily, I would agree with you, Mr. Morton, but from what your wife has just said, I'm getting the impression that she suspects Brad of some kind of foul play. Am I right?"

James squeezed his wife's hand firmer than before. "My wife is upset, Inspector. Please don't let what you have read into her reaction distract you in any way from finding our daughter. You name me one family who doesn't fall out periodically."

Miranda nodded, accepting his reasoning, which still left a niggling doubt gnawing at her insides. She made a mental note to look into things when she got back to the station. "When was the last time you spoke to your daughter?"

"Yesterday. We rang her during the day. It's a stressful time for her right now, what with the launch only a few days away."

"And what frame of mind was she in, apart from her stress load being excessive?" Miranda asked.

Mrs. Morton answered, "Fine. She was stressed, yes, but also very, very excited. When I spoke to her, she was just totting up to give the caterers the final numbers for the after-launch party."

"I see. Please forgive me for asking this—supposing we don't find your daughter in time, will the launch go ahead?"

Mrs. Morton shook her head. "Why should it? How could it? Anneka *is* the brand. Only she can carry off something as huge as this. Only my daughter is capable of doing that, Inspector. That's why it's imperative that we find her quickly. What do you think has happened to her, honestly?"

Miranda pulled in a large breath and let it pass through her lips slowly. "Well, to me, it looks like your daughter might have been abducted."

"What? Why would anyone do that?" James asked, tears welling up in his tired, grey eyes.

Miranda was glad that the upstairs had been cordoned off completely before the couple's arrival. She would have had a devil of a job convincing them that their daughter was alive if they had seen the huge pool of blood on the bathroom floor. "My suspicions are firmly planted in one direction at the moment, with the launch. It's just too much of a coincidence to be anything else. I've asked Brad to give me a list of contacts connected with your daughter's business. We'll be working through that list and interviewing people as soon as possible."

"Do you mind if I look at that list, Inspector? My son-in-law really doesn't have a clue with regard to the business my daughter and I set up over ten years ago."

Miranda glanced across the hallway to her partner, who was busy ringing people on the list, making appointments. "Just a second. I'll get it for you now. I wasn't aware that you used to be involved in the running of the business, Mrs. Morton. Perhaps you could step back in and take over the launch. Would that be possible?"

James spoke for his wife before she had the chance to open her mouth. "No, it wouldn't be possible. My wife has a weak heart, and the stress would likely kill her. I won't allow her to get involved in the business again. Jessica, Anneka's assistant—or personal assistant, call her what you will—is more than capable of taking over that side of things."

That statement alone added another name to Miranda's list of suspects. An extraordinary amount of envy flew around in the corporate world. All Anneka's PA would need to do was make a call to one of Anneka's competitors, offering to divulge secret information in exchange for a sizeable payoff. Miranda put aside that snippet for the time being and made a mental note to look into Jessica's background thoroughly before the day was out.

"Johnny, have you got that list, please?" she called over her shoulder. Turning to the couple again, she added, "I'm sure she is. I'll give her a call later or drop by the office to see her in person, to let her know how important it is that the launch should still go ahead, in spite of Anneka's disappearance. That is what your daughter would want, isn't it?"

Her partner handed the list to Miranda, who then passed it on to Mrs. Morton to peruse. "You look puzzled. What's wrong?"

"At a quick glance, I can see at least five or six names not on this list. You say Brad wrote this out for you?"

"Yes, he used your daughter's address book to create the list. To be fair, he was a little shaken up at the time."

"Foolish man. That's no excuse. I can see immediately that he's left off some of Anneka's biggest rivals. That's just typical of him."

"If you can add to the list, then that would be wonderful and save us a lot of time. I also asked Brad to put a tick alongside anyone who had visited the house. If you would kindly do the same, I'd appreciate it."

"Why on earth would that come into your investigation, Inspector?" James Morton asked, frowning.

Miranda thought fast on her feet. "Well, as the incident took place here, I presume the suspect, or suspects, knew where your daughter lived." She had no intention of upsetting Anneka's parents by telling them about the disabled surveillance equipment or the missing rug, which they had understandably neglected to notice themselves upon their arrival. If they had noticed, they hadn't voiced their observations.

Mrs. Morton spent the next five minutes adding to the list then handed it back to Miranda.

"That's fantastic. I'm afraid I need to go back to the station now and get ready for the conference."

"Conference? What conference? To do with the case, you mean?" James Morton asked.

"It's more of an appeal, really. Brad will be there. He might be too upset to speak, so I've volunteered to make a plea on his behalf. He is still considering his options on that."

"Is there any chance that we could be part of the appeal, Inspector? I wouldn't want to step on anyone's toes, but I think Sheila and I have the right, more than enough rights, as Anneka's parents, to be involved fully in this investigation. After all, she was our daughter long before she ever married him." James seemed as annoyed by Brad as his wife had earlier on in the conversation.

"Of course. I'd be willing to involve you without hesitation on my part. To be honest, experience shows us that the more people who get involved in the appeal, the better. It'll prove to the general public how much your daughter is loved and missed."

"What time is it due to take place?" James asked, quickly squeezing his wife's hands again.

"At four this afternoon. Brad will be at the station around three thirty. Umm… if there is any animosity between you, I'm begging you to suppress it for now, at least until Anneka is found. It would be better for all parties concerned to get along with each other until the case has been solved. In the past, I've had to deal with similar cases where feuding families have only tended to hamper our investigation."

James nodded. "You have our word on that, Inspector. Doesn't she, love?"

Reluctantly, Sheila Morton gave her husband a tearful smile and said quietly, "Yes, I give you my word to call a truce with Brad for the time being."

"Good. Can you give me a contact number where I can reach you? I'll do my very best to keep you up to date on things."

Sheila opened her bag and withdrew one of her old cards associated with her daughter's business. Miranda accepted it and showed the couple out of the house. Then she closed the door and pressed her back against the wall.

"Everything all right, boss?" Johnny asked from the lounge doorway.

"That, my dear partner, remains to be seen."

CHAPTER FOUR

The following few hours passed Miranda by with lightning speed. She organised the team to go through the list of possible suspects, actioned the investigation into any past grievances out there in the public domain, then got on with the tasks she wanted to carry out personally before three thirty came around.

She picked up the phone and placed a call. "Hello, Miss Tomasson? This is Detective Inspector Miranda Carr. If you have five minutes, I'd like a chat with you."

"I don't, not now, Inspector. What is it in connection with anyway?" Miss Tomasson's tone was a mixture of surprise and harassment.

"The disappearance of your boss. I realise how busy you are. However, this is now a police investigation, and anything else must be put aside right now."

"I can't do that! Anneka would kill me."

"I have an appeal with the media and press arranged for this afternoon, after which I intend coming to your place of work to see you, Miss Tomasson. If that's an inconvenience, then tough. It's urgent that I find your boss as soon as possible, given the circumstances."

The woman gave a guttural growl. "I'm not with you. What circumstances?"

"I can't and won't go into that sort of detail over the phone. I do appreciate you have a launch party to arrange and the pressures that must entail. All I'm asking is that you schedule me in for ten minutes of your valuable time."

"Very well. Come to the office at six. I'm planning to squeeze in something to eat around that time. If you don't mind me talking through a mouthful of takeaway, be my guest."

"Thank you, that's very accommodating of you. I'll see you then."

Miranda hung up, relieved she had persuaded the woman to see her without being too heavy-handed. She picked up her post and worked through the more important letters until mid-afternoon.

The phone rang on her desk. "Yes, DI Carr."

"Ma'am, it's the duty sergeant. I have a Mr. Lawrence here wanting to see you."

"Thanks. Tell him to take a seat, and I'll be with him in a moment, Fred."

Miranda hung up, unhitched her jacket off the back of her chair, and left the office. "Johnny, I'm going down to greet Brad Lawrence and to see how things are shaping up for the conference. Are you going to join me downstairs or carry on up here?"

Johnny looked up from his computer screen and shrugged. "I don't mind. Do you think things will kick off between the husband and parents?"

"I hope not. They've been warned. Stay here then and carry on with the background checks, all right?"

"Suits me. I'm just delving into Jessica's background now in readiness for the meeting later."

"Great. I didn't get a chance to do that myself. What would I do without you? I'll see you in an hour or so, I hope."

Johnny beamed at her then turned back to the screen.

Miranda made her way to the station's reception area. She stood there for a second or two, watching Brad Lawrence, gauging his demeanour before announcing her arrival. He seemed relatively relaxed compared to how he'd been the last time she laid eyes on him.

"Who are you spying on?"

Miranda spun around sharply and slapped a hand over her erratically beating heart.

"Cause a girl a heart attack, why don't you, chief?" Miranda shook her head at the smirk on her best friend's face.

Detective Chief Inspector Caroline Gordon brushed her long brown hair over her shoulder and peeked through the small window herself. "Don't tell me you didn't hear my size sixes coming down the hallway? You must have been too engrossed in eyeing up that handsome creature in there."

"Yeah, if that was the case, Alan would dump me before the vicar had a chance to schedule the service."

The two women laughed.

"No, seriously. Is he the missing woman's husband?"

"Yep. It's been a hectic day. Sorry I haven't kept you up to date with things."

The chief waved a forgiving hand. "It's early days yet. So"—she aimed a thumb in Lawrence's direction—"do you think he's done it?"

"I'm not getting that impression, but as you so rightly pointed out, it's early days yet. Let's see how he performs during the appeal and then re-evaluate his part afterwards, shall we?"

"Sounds like a plan. Talking of vicars, how are the wedding plans coming along?"

"Oh, you know, the usual family shit flying around. 'I'm not going to attend if Auntie Grace goes. Don't expect me to turn up if Uncle Derek is invited.' Just what is wrong with people? Why can't anyone take the bride and groom's feelings into consideration? To be frank with you, I've had enough of it all, so much so that I'm considering asking Alan if he wants to take off somewhere to elope."

Caroline grabbed her arms. "You can't do that! I'll never forgive you."

Miranda chortled. "No pressure there then. Why won't you forgive me?"

"Because I've just spent a bloody fortune on buying a hat for the occasion."

"Crap. Really? Are you trying to give Cilla a run for her money in those stakes?"

"Hardly. I bought a swanky new silk suit for the occasion, too. Can't let my good buddy down by turning up in the ten-year-old suit, the one usually set aside for such occasions, can I? Anyway, I saw the suit in a cute boutique in Chelsea, and there, sitting alongside it, was a matching clutch-bag and pillbox hat. I couldn't resist them. Can you imagine how much I forked out for such perfection? So don't even think of running away to get hitched or..."

"Or what? You'll demote me? Hah, you wouldn't dare. I'm the best DI around, and you damn well know it."

The chief slapped her thigh. "Damn, why do you always have to throw that one at me when we're having an argument?"

"Firstly, I wasn't aware that we *were* arguing, and secondly, because it's the bloody *truth*."

Caroline raised her hands and winked at Miranda. "Fair enough. Back to business. Are you all set?"

"Yep, I think so. I'm just waiting for the parents to..." Miranda stopped speaking when Sheila and James Morton marched up to the reception desk. "This should be interesting."

"What should?"

"Well, that's Anneka's parents. I want you to see how they react to Brad and give me your take on things before I tell you what I know."

The two women watched the interaction in the adjacent room.

Caroline shuddered. "I'm picking up on a distinct chill in the air."

"Yeah, that's what I'm getting, too, especially from the parents when they talk about the dear hubby. Not so much when Brad was talking about them, though."

"Do you think they suspect him?"

Miranda shook her head. "I don't think so at this point, although they have thrown out some pretty major hints that they can't stand the man. I've yet to have all three in the same room together, but now I've had the privilege of seeing that, I'd say their animosity towards each other could end up damaging this case. I just hope they can control themselves during the appeal. I've invited them all to say their piece to the camera."

Caroline snorted. "You do insist on making your life difficult at times, dear, don't you?"

"Funny. Let's hope, for all our sakes, they keep their emotions in check. You'll be there, won't you?"

"Wouldn't miss it for the world. The last boxing match I saw involved Mike Tyson. What a bloody affair that turned out to be."

"God, don't say that! Hey, you're showing your age again," Miranda pulled her friend's leg. "If you'll excuse me, I better step in there before things get too heated. I'm not liking the body language I'm picking up from either party."

"I'll drop back five minutes before the appeal is due to start. I need to make myself look beautiful before then."

Miranda looked at her watch. "Impossible, you've only got fifteen minutes. You'd need at least fifteen years to complete that improvement."

Caroline Gordon swept her hair over her slender shoulder à la Miss Piggy and stormed off without saying another word.

"Hello, Brad. Mr. and Mrs. Morton. Would you like to come with me, please?" The three people smiled briefly and followed her up the narrow, echoing hallway to the room at the rear of the building. The room, set aside for this specific purpose, was being used more and more on Miranda's patch. She personally was dying to put an end to that. However, with crime rates escalating in the London area, she knew the likelihood of seeing that happen before she retired was virtually zero.

Miranda spent the next few minutes preparing the family for what was about to take place. Much to the annoyance of Anneka's parents, Brad chose that time to back out of making the appeal. However, they held their tongues and didn't berate him, much to Miranda's relief. The chief joined them, and any awkwardness the group felt dissolved quickly.

After the introductions were made, Julie Shaw, the person in charge of organising the press and media, asked them all to take a seat behind the long table draped in a white cloth with the Metropolitan Police emblem on the front.

DCI Gordon conducted the appeal from her seat next to Miranda. She told the viewers who the victim was and where she was last seen then asked the public for their assistance in finding Anneka Lawrence. The chief didn't mention how much blood the victim had likely lost and that everyone should be on the lookout for a corpse, rather than Anneka walking the streets, looking lost, dazed, and confused.

"Inspector Carr is in charge of the investigation." Once she had divulged the crucial details and stressed the urgency of the situation, Caroline handed the baton over to Miranda.

"Thank you, ma'am. We have Anneka's parents, who have abandoned their holiday to return home to help in the search for their daughter, and her husband. Brad Lawrence, is too distraught to make an appeal right now himself. Therefore, I will be reading what he's eager to say on his behalf." Miranda turned to Brad and gave him a reassuring smile. She cleared her throat then read from the sheet of paper he'd presented to her upon his arrival. "Please, please, please, whoever has my wife, I'm begging you not to hurt her. Let her go without causing her any further discomfort. We'll pay any kind of ransom, just as long as we get Anneka back safe and sound. She is my best friend, the pulse that keeps me alive and breathing. Please, return her to us immediately. We all miss her dearly."

During the speech, Miranda noticed out of the corner of her eye that Brad had buried his head in his hands. Anneka's parents were looking at him angrily and shaking their heads, not bothering to hide their distaste for the man from the public eye. Miranda asked Anneka's parents if they would like to add a few words of their own.

Both Sheila and James nodded and clung to each other's hands. However, it was James who spoke to the camera. Miranda had expected Sheila to break down in tears as Brad had while Miranda read his heartfelt speech, but nothing could have been farther from the truth.

"Our daughter has a kind soul, the kindest soul I've ever seen in a person. Even though she is a very successful businesswoman, she has never forgotten her roots. She's our pride and joy, our only child, and we're keen to have her returned to us unharmed. Please, whatever you need in exchange for giving our beautiful daughter back to us, you only have to ask. We love her dearly and are awaiting the day when we will be reunited with our baby. If anyone knows anything at all of Anneka's whereabouts, please contact Inspector Carr and her team immediately. Anneka, we love you, sweetheart. You're our heart and soul. We'll never lose hope of finding and bringing you home. Stay strong, darling. We're doing everything in our power to find you."

DCI Gordon cleared her throat and drew the appeal to a close. "Let's hope your plea hit a note with the abductor, Mr. and Mrs. Morton. I applaud you for having the strength to speak out so eloquently at such a distressing time."

"Thank you." James Morton shook the chief's hand and stood up. Glancing Miranda's way, he added, "Please do anything and everything you can to bring this case to a swift conclusion, Inspector, one way or another. And, Brad, you can quit the crocodile tears now. The camera has stopped rolling. You, my boy, should be out there, searching for our daughter day and night, but I know in my heart that just isn't going to happen. I hope, for once in your life, you manage to break down the selfish barrier your parents gave you and find it within to put Anneka's needs first. She *needs* you to be out there looking for her twenty-four-seven. Shake off that self-pity and prioritise someone else's needs for a change."

Miranda cringed, and she could tell by the way the DCI's mouth was gaping open that Caroline was flabbergasted. During the dressing down, Brad stared at his clenched hands rather than making eye contact with James Morton. Miranda's mind started racing, and she found herself eager to press on with the investigation. But first, she would need to bid farewell to Anneka's parents and husband, for a while, anyhow.

"If you'd like to come this way, I'll show you out." She shook hands with the parents first. "The phone lines are always red-hot for the first few days after this type of appeal goes out. We're bound to get calls coming in from the length and breadth of the UK. It'll take us time to sift through those calls. Be assured that my team will be working on this case night and day until Anneka is found."

"Thank you, Inspector. Please keep us informed as the investigation progresses. Do not hesitate to get in touch with us if we can be of assistance in any way. We'll only be stuck at home, twiddling our fingers, sitting by the phone anyway."

"I will keep you in the loop—you have my guarantee on that. One last thing, I ask of you, please try and stay positive throughout the investigation."

"You have our word on that," James assured her. He opened the door and motioned for his wife to leave the building ahead of him. Miranda smiled, noting that James seemed to be from the old school where men knew how to treat women well. Maybe part of the reason he had taken Brad to task after the appeal was that he expected Brad to uphold his same standards for treating women properly.

Miranda shook hands with Brad, noticing how hot and clammy his palm was. "I'll be in touch in the next few days. If you think of anything else we should know about in the meantime, please call me any hour of the day or night, okay?"

In a subdued tone, Brad replied, "I will, Inspector. Good luck finding my wife."

Miranda stood by the entrance and observed while the man got in his vehicle and drove out of the car park, her insides constricting. She ran up the stairs to the incident room.

"Have the phones started ringing yet?" she asked the team.

Johnny looked puzzled, as if she had lost her mind. "Er... are you forgetting that the appeal hasn't aired yet, boss?"

"Crap, crap, crap! What is wrong with me?" She kicked a chair and sent it hurtling across the room. Then she noted the time on her watch. "All right, stupid me. Johnny, we're due at the PA's office at six. That leaves us an hour to dig up some dirt on the husband. Anything and everything we can find."

"Really? Is that the way the investigation is heading? You think the hubby did it?"

She placed a hand over her flat stomach. "That's what my gut is telling me, whether we can find the bloody evidence to back that up is a totally different ballgame. Let's give it a go, eh?"

"Sure. I'll make a start. Do you just want me to do a quick search for recent activity that might show up, or should I go way back?"

"Let's keep things recent for now, due to lack of time. You can dig deeper when we resume work in the morning. How's that?"

Johnny headed for his desk and threw himself in his chair, already tapping his keyboard before his backside reached the seat.

Miranda grabbed a coffee from the vending machine and entered her office just as the phone rang on her desk. "DI Carr."

"It's me."

Reclining in her chair, she grinned when she heard her fiancé's sexy voice. "Hello, Me! I was just about to ring you. Is everything all right?"

"Yep, I'm finishing work early today. My last client cancelled her appointment."

"There's a surprise. Maybe the thought of having three fillings was enough to send her running for cover. I know I would if I were in her shoes."

"Yeah, good job you get all your treatment for free. Not sure many people can afford to visit the dentist any longer. Our client list is getting less and less since the damn prices went up."

"I'm sure things will pick up soon, sweetie. Put it down to the current economic climate. Blame the corrupt bankers for getting the country in the shit."

"All right, love. Didn't mean to start you off on one of your rants. I was going to drop by the supermarket on the way home. What do you fancy for dinner tonight?"

"Sorry. Let me think… after the day I've had, I'd love a blowout meal. Sod the diet for a day or two."

He chuckled. "I knew the wedding-dress diet would falter soon enough."

"Cheek! Some *nice* people I know would tear me off a strip or two for even contemplating losing weight before the wedding. I'll have you know I'm the same size now as when I left school."

"Did they have physical exercise in your day at school then?"

"You wait! You'll suffer for that uncalled-for comment before the evening is out, Alan Rogers."

"Oooh… promises, promises. Back to the shopping—why don't we compromise and have steak and salad. I'll go easy on the dressing. How does that sound?"

"Wonderful. You do spoil me. I hope that doesn't change when you slip that ring on my finger."

"Fat chance of that happening. You wouldn't allow it, for a start."

"Ain't that the truth? Look, I've got a meeting with someone in the city centre at six. I should be clear around six thirty at the latest. Depending on the traffic, I should be home about seven to seven thirty. Do me a favour and pick up a couple of bottles of chardonnay, will you? I'll settle up with you when I get home."

"Yeah, right. How many times have I heard that lately? Er… just a reminder that wine contains calories, too, soon-to-be Mrs. Rogers. I'll see if there's a low-cal equivalent."

"Don't you dare! That's the one bloody luxury I have left," she cried, incensed, before adding in a whiny voice, "You wouldn't begrudge your beloved a teeny-weeny glass of wine just to help me unwind after a long arduous day, would you?"

"Stop that! I'm being hard because you told me to be hard on you. I'm marrying you for who you are, tiny fat lumps and all. Oh crap, I really shouldn't have said that, should I?"

"No, soon-to-be dearest husband. I'm going to enjoy getting my revenge later. Okay, I've gotta fly. Love you, despite you not liking my fat lumps."

"I never said that. Love you, too. See you later." Alan blew her a kiss down the line, as he always did.

Miranda replaced the phone and sat back with a soppy grin stretching her mouth apart. Before long, the phone rang again. She snatched it up, and in her sexiest voice, she said, "What did you forget, lover boy?"

"The last time I looked in the mirror, I was definitely female. I had no idea you had a leaning towards wanting to go to bed with me."

"Oh, crap. Sorry, wrong sex. Sorry, Chief." She cringed at her faux pas.

"How is that gorgeous man of yours?"

"He's great. He called to see what I wanted for dinner. I thought he was ringing back after forgetting to tell me something."

"Ain't he sweet? You need to hang on to that one, girlie."

"I intend to. What can I do for you, Caroline?" Sometimes Miranda forgot herself and called her good friend a mixture of names when they were alone. She was more conscious of addressing her superior correctly when they were in the company of others, though.

"Nothing really. I just wanted your impressions on how the appeal went."

"Let's just say it's prompted me to start looking into the husband's background. Of course, I would have done that within the next few days anyway. I always do in these kinds of cases. But his reactions today had me worried from the start."

"Yep, I got that impression, too. Keep me informed on this one, Miranda. This is a high profile case, after all."

"Leave it with me, gov," she reassured the chief. Miranda hung up, glad she had a good relationship with her superior and that Caroline always left her to get on with her job without any unnecessary interference. Over the years, she'd heard several horror stories from work associates, particularly female inspectors, working with male DCIs who questioned every detail in a case rather than trusting the inspector's abilities. However, God help anyone who crossed Chief Gordon. When vexed and pushed to the limit, she had a tendency to tear into people for doing the most harmless of things. Despite the easy-going nature she emanated to her colleagues daily, she definitely didn't put up with incompetence on the job.

Johnny knocked on the door and walked into the office, his expression unreadable, even to Miranda's expert eye. He lowered himself into the chair opposite her and waved a piece of paper in his hand. "Up till now, I haven't really found much in the way of dirt on Brad Lawrence. What I did manage to find out was that he started up an executive travel company a few years back. You know the kind of thing—chartered jets and yachts, mainly jets by the look of things. He's a qualified pilot and flew the plane himself."

"Interesting. Maybe that's how they met."

"Could be. I dare say I can find that out if I dig deep enough. Time's getting on, and I wasn't sure if you were aware of that. I can carry on with this tomorrow if you want to head out. There's the rush-hour traffic to consider."

"What would I do without you to state the obvious for me, Johnny?" She smiled and winked at her partner. "I'm ready now anyway. The chief just rang to get my impression on Lawrence. I told her we were looking into that side of things. Hey, you never know, perhaps we'll strike lucky with Anneka's PA."

"In what way? Dishing the dirt on their marriage?"

"That's exactly what I'm thinking. Come on. Let's go. Have we got enough people manning the phones tonight?"

"All organised. Craig has volunteered to stay until nine, and then the desk sergeant said he'd make sure his staff cover the phones until we come back in the morning."

"That's great." Miranda gathered her jacket and handbag, hoping to head off home straight after they finished the interview with the PA. "What about your car?"

"I'll leave it here and get the tube in the morning."

"That makes sense. Let's get a wriggle on." After making sure the rest of the team knew what was expected of them before they finished work in the next half an hour or so, Miranda left the station with Johnny in tow. "Programme the sat nav, will you?" Miranda asked, putting her bag in the backseat and removing her jacket once again.

Johnny punched in the address, and they set off. Before long, they found themselves nose to tail on one of the B-roads on the outskirts of the city.

"Doesn't that thing ever come up with a suitable shortcut?" She asked, drumming her fingers on the steering wheel.

"It should do. I'm not sure how it reads the levels of congestion, though." Johnny shrugged. He wasn't really tech savvy at the best of times and was even less so with the new sat navs the force had just rolled out to all their superior officers.

Patience proved to be their greatest friend over the next twenty minutes as the traffic ebbed and flowed around the city. "Whew, five minutes to spare. I didn't think we were ever going to make it."

Johnny pointed out the entrance to the underground car park beneath the office block they were after. "Here we are. At least we know your car will be safe."

"There is that. What's the betting the lift is out of action and the office we're after is on the top floor?"

"You ain't catching me out on that one. You're usually right about these sorts of things."

A security guard was standing alongside the lift when they pushed open the door. "Can I help?" the man's voice was deep, and he had a thick cockney accent.

Miranda showed her ID. "We're after Eternal Youth Cosmetics head office. Please don't tell me it's on the top floor."

The man grinned, showing off large gaps in his teeth. "Yep, it's a penthouse office. Hey, you're in luck—the engineers came to fix the lift shaft today. It's been out of action for over a week."

They climbed aboard the lift and thanked the guard for his help. "Makes a change for something to go our way," Miranda announced appreciatively when the lift jerked into action.

The doors slid back after the swift ascent and opened onto a carpeted hallway. The door at the end indicated they had come to the right floor. Miranda knocked and pushed open the door to find an attractive secretary, who greeted her with a well-practised welcoming smile.

Again, Miranda flashed her ID. "We're here to see Jessica."

"Ah yes, take a seat. I'll see if she's free to see you."

The woman left the reception area and returned with another woman in her mid-to-late twenties. Dark circles rimmed her eyes, and the brief smile she offered appeared exhausted, too. She shook hands with the two detectives and instructed them to follow her into the office. "This is Anneka's office. She adores looking out on that skyline, especially in the winter, when the nights draw in early. Have you heard from her?"

The three of them sat down either side of the large mahogany desk in the spacious office. Miranda shook her head. "No, nothing. That was going to be my first question to you."

Jessica picked up a pen and started twisting it through her long slender fingers. "Unfortunately not."

"I appreciate you seeing us at such short notice during what must be one of the most stressful times in your calendar, but you understand how important it is to find Anneka before too much time elapses, don't you? The longer we delay, the greater the risk of circumstances getting out of hand, if you know what I mean."

"I do understand, and, yes, this is a very hectic time. I can only spare you fifteen minutes, at the most, Inspector."

"That's fine. I need to ask a few probing questions about the Lawrences' marriage. Did Anneka share any insight into her personal life?"

After a knock on the door, the secretary walked in, accompanied by the smell of Chinese takeaway. "Thanks, Sandy. Can we get you a drink, detectives?"

"No, thanks all the same. Please go ahead and eat while we talk." The scenario wasn't ideal, but if she had to choose between spending ten minutes watching the young woman stuff her face and not being there, then she was willing to accept it.

They waited until the secretary left the room then resumed the conversation.

To Miranda's disappointment, Jessica appeared to be more intent on tucking into her meal than answering the question about Anneka's marriage. Miranda was just about to prompt the woman when the young woman looked up and locked gazes with her.

"Sometimes. I think they've been going through a rough patch lately. How much of that was due to the pressure of the new product launch, I have no idea." She took a mouthful of beef and noodles, chewed it a little, and carried on. "She confided in me a few weeks back that Brad's been spending more and more time away from home."

Miranda looked at her partner and raised an eyebrow. "Did she mention why or where he was?"

"She put it under the umbrella of him searching for work. He just seemed to be away a lot to me. Don't people tend to use their phones more nowadays? I just thought it was odd that he would frequently tell her he would be away for a few days, seeing a contact for a possible investment opportunity."

"By that, I take it you think he was having an affair?"

"The thing is, Inspector, I think only he can answer that. In my mind, he's not likely to own up to anything like that while Anneka is missing, is he?"

"Oh, don't worry. We'll be sure to ask the question when we next see him. So, would you say their marriage had totally derailed or only briefly come off the tracks?"

"I can't answer that as an outsider. All I can say is that Anneka was happy working long hours sometimes rather than going back home."

"Interesting. The obvious question is, do you know if their marriage could be regarded as violent or abusive?"

She shrugged and chewed on another piece of beef as she thought. "Not sure. If she was physically abused, then I never really saw any signs of that. She didn't come to work with any black eyes from what I can remember."

"It's not uncommon for abusers to attack their victims' torsos, where everyday clothing will hide the proof. Most friends and family members are unaware of their loved ones going through an unimaginable hell until it's too late to do anything about it."

Jessica's fork dropped onto her noodles. "Are you saying that you think Brad might have killed her and disposed of the body?" she asked incredulously.

Miranda laughed internally at the woman's phrasing. She was obviously a keen mystery watcher. "It's a little early to start casting aspersions like that around, Miss Tomasson, but it is something that we intend to look into in the immediate future. Anything you can tell us, any possible secrets that Anneka confided in you perhaps, will be treated with the utmost confidentiality. You have my word on that.

"Apart from what I've already told you, there's very little I can share, Inspector. I did tell Anneka on more than one occasion that she should get rid of Brad."

"And her response to that was?"

"That she loved him, in spite of his numerous faults."

"Did Anneka ever have cause to doubt her husband's love for her?"

"No. I think she foolishly believed he loved her wholeheartedly and without doubts."

Miranda sighed deeply. "So, you think that Anneka thought her husband was having an affair or plural affairs, but she was still in denial. So she threw herself into working longer hours to avoid being presented with the truth, is that it?"

"That's it exactly. Although she would never admit to it, of course. Sometimes she breezed around here like she was in her own little bubble. Inspector, what if her bubble has now burst? Do you think we'll ever see her again?" Sadness filled the PA's eyes, and she pushed her half-finished meal towards the edge of the table.

"Your guess is as good as mine on that front, Jessica. There's an appeal due to go out during the local evening news and in the paper tonight. We're hoping to gain some information from that—possible sightings or maybe even a confession from an intruder who wants to admit that things got out of hand when he broke into the Lawrences' property. It's not unheard of for a culprit's conscience to prick in such cases. Admittedly, it's unusual, but 'Never say never' is my motto on that front."

"Can I ask what makes you think there was an intruder in the house?"

"Let's just say that the evidence we've been provided initially led us to believe that. However, given what you've just told us"—Jessica opened her mouth to object, and Miranda raised her hand to stop her—"and other things that have come to light since the appeal took place this afternoon, I believe our investigation will be veering off in another direction altogether soon. Between you and us, Jessica, there was an awful lot of blood found at the house, in the en suite bathroom, in fact, which leads us to think that Anneka was violently attacked before she went missing."

"Oh my God. When I hung up last night, she was about to unwind in the bath. Maybe she was distracted by my call and forgot to lock the front door before she got in the tub. Poor Anneka." Tears formed and spilled onto her cheeks.

"You rang last night?"

"She rang me, gave me instructions for the evening. I haven't been home since yesterday morning. That's why I look a wreck."

"I see. Can you tell me if she sounded distressed in any way? As though someone was with her when she made the call?"

"No! My God, did the call distract her, do you think? We were running through some final details for the launch."

"Please, don't start blaming yourself for this. Let's just hope we find Anneka alive and well in the next few hours or days." Miranda rose from her seat, and Johnny did the same. "We'll leave you to it then. Good luck with the launch. Is everything going to plan now?"

"It seems to be. I've been implementing Anneka's instructions all day. It's still going to take me a few more days to conclude those instructions. People have no idea what it takes to launch something as major as this."

"I'm sure. One final question, if I may? Brad and Anneka's mother gave us a list of rivals who might have had some sort of vendetta and might set out to disrupt the launch. We'll be looking into that list starting tomorrow. I just wondered, what with you working so closely with Anneka, if you could tell us if anything untoward has taken place recently. In that I mean, has she had any cause to publicly fall out with anyone from any of these firms?"

"I can't think of anything off the top of my head. There's always some snide remark made now and again, but nothing that would cause me enough concern to inform you. Envy is in every crevice in this industry, I'm afraid. I've heard it's even worse on the designer clothing circuit. Now that would definitely not appeal to me."

"You've been very generous with your time and your insight into your boss's working and personal life. I appreciate that, Jess. I'll be in touch if I need any further information, should something else crop up, if that's okay?"

"Of course. Please do what you can to bring Anneka home where she belongs." Jessica left her chair and showed them out to the outer office door.

"We'll do our best. One last thing—what will happen to the business now? If Anneka doesn't return, let's put it that way?" Miranda asked, scrutinising the young woman's reaction.

"I really don't know. I suppose either Brad or Sheila will take over the day-to-day running of things alongside me. Damn, I hadn't thought of that." The woman looked terrified by the thought.

"Sorry to leave you with such a dilemma. Try not to worry too much about that side of things for now, you have enough on your plate as it is. Let's see if we can find Anneka so that scenario doesn't rear its head."

The detectives shook hands with the woman. During the elevator ride back down to the basement, they mulled over the information gathered from the meeting.

"Again, I sense the finger being pointed firmly in Brad's direction, don't you?"

"Hmm… it certainly seems that way to me, boss. If the business was about to be handed over to Jessica back there, however, my money would be on her doing the deed."

"What? Are you serious, man?"

"Why not? She'd have a lot to gain. She also knew that Anneka was in the house alone and about to get in the bath."

Miranda snorted. "What does that prove?"

"I don't know. I'm just putting all the facts out there. I did say if there was a chance of the business falling into her hands, that kind of consequence was possible."

"Yeah, but it's not. That pleasure, if Anneka is dead, falls to either Sheila or Brad. My money is on Sheila taking over the reins, given the amount of resentment she's carrying for Brad and the fact that she created the business alongside her daughter anyway."

"Agreed. So, what are we going to do about Brad?"

"First thing in the morning, I'm going to pay him a visit. Let's hope we get plenty of calls to sieve through tonight before we tackle him again. I need facts, dates, times, and sightings to fire at him. I get the impression we'll be comparing him to a wriggly worm soon."

"Huh?" Johnny grunted.

"He's going to prove a slippery character. I think from this day forward, we should take anything he says with a pinch of salt."

"Do you think he married her for her money with the intention of bumping her off?"

Miranda shrugged her weary shoulders and leaned back against the glass wall of the lift. "I'm not sure about that. If he did, why would he do it now and not wait until after the big launch. Surely that would make more sense, once the money from the new range started registering at the tills, yes?"

"I guess. Can you drop me off at the tube station on your way through?"

"Of course. Let's put our heads together tomorrow and draw up a list of probable motives."

Johnny shook his head and tutted. "Yeah, right, like that's going to happen."

"Meaning?"

"Meaning that you'll probably spend the evening drawing up a schedule for tomorrow."

"If I did that, Alan would kill me. Anyway, there's no point doing it tonight. We need to see what kind of response the appeal brings in first."

They had reached the car by then. "I can't see it throwing much our way, to be honest," Johnny said across the top of the car before getting in. "I'm happy to be proved wrong, of course."

Miranda got behind the steering wheel. "You know what, partner? On this one, I'm inclined to agree with you."

She dropped Johnny off at the station a few miles down the road and continued on her journey home, her mind constantly replaying the day's many events.

"Hi, sweetheart, I'm home at last," she called out as she entered the front door.

Alan draped his athletic frame against the lounge doorway and beamed at her. She walked forward and melted into his arms. They shared one of their extra-special 'welcome home' kisses. They'd made a pact when they had first moved into their three-bedroomed, terraced home that no matter how crappy their days were, they always spent the first ten minutes showing how much they meant to each other. So far, everything had gone according to plan, but ever the pessimist, Miranda often found herself wondering if the rings they were about to put on their fingers would alter that after a few months or years.

"Bad day at the office, love?" Alan asked after their cuddle session was over and they had gone through to the kitchen.

"Yes and no. More frustrating than anything, I'd guess you'd call it. You? How many extractions did you carry out?" Miranda winked; it was the only procedure she ever enquired about.

Smiling, Alan shook his head. "Same old question. The trouble is you see my role as a paid torture expert, don't you? Go on, be honest."

"You be honest—you love it when people sit in your chair and you see their knuckles turn white and their legs frantically wiggling."

Alan laughed. "Maybe. Hey, a man's got to get his kicks somehow, eh?"

And that was Alan in a nutshell, her deliciously handsome fiancé at his best. Ever reliable for making light of a situation, he was never one to take life or his family and friends for granted. Miranda felt blessed to be marrying the all-around nice guy. Since their first meeting—at a nightclub, of all places—they had been virtually inseparable. They were alike in so many ways. He was her best friend, and from the beginning, she had shared so many secrets and life's ambitions with him that she'd never shared with anyone else but her parents. They understood each other perfectly. They weren't one of those couples who had to try hard to come up with special events to keep the spark alive in their relationship. Theirs just happened naturally.

Saying that, the last few months of contending with wedding arrangements on top of their very busy careers had introduced a few tetchy moments into their relationship. Thankfully, both had realised what was going on as soon as it cropped up, and they laughed off the tension as a bad joke. It was a cliché, she knew, but she always told people that they were born to be together—soul mates who had loved one another in a previous life.

"Just make sure you don't bring that side of your work home with you. Or I might have to get my handcuffs out and think up a little role-playing of my own."

His eyebrow rose. "Is it wrong for me to like the sound of that suggestion?"

Miranda sat on the barstool at the end of the worktop and roared with laughter. "Is dinner nearly ready?"

"Ah, the sound of yet another conversation being changed because of dubious subject matter."

"Just answer the question and stop trying to embarrass me."

"Yep, I've just got to grill the steak, and we're good to go. Do you want to pour us both a glass of wine?"

"So you succumbed in the end?"

"Oh yes, you can't have steak without a little wine on the side. You should know that by now. I don't suppose you had a chance to look through the list of florists?"

Miranda stopped in her tracks, mid-reach for the glasses. "Damn, sorry. I forgot. Or rather I didn't have time what with this new case surfacing first thing this morning."

"Never mind. Actually, while I was drilling in a client's mouth today, I came up with a great idea. Shoot it down if you don't agree."

She opened the bottle and began pouring the wine. "Go on."

"What about getting your mum and dad to do the flowers?"

Miranda pondered the suggestion then smiled. "I love the idea. We're still going to stick with our original plan and pay for them, though, right?"

"Of course. I meant what I said. This is our big day, and I don't see why they should foot the bill for it. Tradition sucks at times, especially when the cost of a wedding has now blown up out of all proportion. Businesses have cottoned on to how lucrative weddings can be. Anyway, my thinking is that if your mum and dad's garden centre provides the flowers and plants we need at the church and the reception, it'll go a long way to providing them with some valuable advertising. The fire did more than damage the centre and their stock—it also damaged their reputation insofar as they've been out of action for the past few months. This will make good for some of that damage. What do you think?"

Miranda placed her hand behind his head and pulled him towards her for a kiss. "I think you're a very kind and considerate man, Alan

Rogers, and I can't wait until we tie the knot and make it all official. I'll ring Mum and run it past her after dinner. I have a feeling she'll object initially, but once the idea starts swimming around in her mind, she'll jump on it."

"Good. Let's serve up and eat."

After clearing up together, Miranda was shocked to learn that it was past nine o'clock. "Where the hell has the day gone? I better ring Mum before it gets too late. You know what early birds they are."

"I'll bring a coffee through in a minute."

Miranda settled herself on the sofa, tucked her legs underneath her, and rang her mother.

"Hi, Mum. Sorry to ring so late."

"That's all right, darling. It's always lovely to hear from you. I saw your appeal go out earlier. What a dreadful thing to happen to that woman. She has so much to look forward to with her business doing so well."

"I know, Mum. I have to say it's not looking good, judging by the amount of blood at the scene. We deliberately kept that snippet of information from the public."

Her mother gasped. "Oh my, so you think the woman is dead?" Her mother groaned a little, and it sounded like she needed to sit down due to the shock.

"Sorry, Mum. I shouldn't have told you that. Ignore me. Listen, Alan and I have been chatting over dinner, and I wanted to run something by you with regards to the wedding."

"Oh no, not more bad news! You're not going to elope or, even worse, call it off, are you?"

Miranda laughed. "Gosh, why hadn't we thought of that? The eloping side of things, I mean. No, we're fine, solid in fact, and we have no intention of ever breaking up."

Alan walked in with two mugs of coffee and pecked her on the cheek. "You have my word on that, Janet. You're all stuck with me, I'm afraid."

Sitting down next to her, Alan leaned over, and Miranda held the phone between them so he could hear her mother's side of the conversation.

"Well, I, for one, wouldn't want you to be involved with anyone else, sweetheart. You see and hear about the most dreadful things on TV of what men have done to their wives or girlfriends. You wouldn't believe some of the things these men subject these women to."

"Er... Mum, I'm a DI in a murder investigation team. I see evidence of that every day of the week, or had you forgotten that?"

"Oh, yes. Silly me. Anyway, getting back to this brilliant idea you were about to share with me. You did say it was a brilliant idea, didn't you? Gosh, I wish my memory would stop playing tricks on me."

"No, I didn't say that. I said Alan and I had been chatting. That's all. But I do think he's come up with a brilliant idea, so maybe you had a premonition on that one."

They all laughed, then Miranda told her mother their idea.

"What an excellent plan. Gosh, why didn't we think of this a few weeks or months back?"

"Because you were tied up with rebuilding after the fire, Mum. Are you sure you and Dad would be able to handle this on top of getting the garden centre open again? I wouldn't want to put extra pressure on you at this time."

"Nonsense. Your father can deal with the business while I take care of you two. Oh, what a thrill it is for you to ask us to do this."

"I was hoping you'd see it that way, Mum. Now, don't go overdoing it. We'll cover the cost between us, Alan and me, but there will have to be a budget you need to adhere to, got that?"

"Oh, yes. One must always stick to one's budget, dear."

"I mean it! Don't start adding bits and carrying the cost yourself. You hear me?"

"I promise, dear. I will be giving you everything at cost price, though. No point in arguing on that one, either. The Mighty Mother has spoken."

"You're nuts. We'll see. How's Dad coping with all the extra work?"

"He's fine. Between us, we're coping better than either of us anticipated. Why don't you and Alan pop over for Sunday lunch, and we can discuss things in more depth then?"

Alan gave her his nod of approval.

"We'd love to. Do you want us to bring anything?"

"A bottle of wine or two wouldn't go amiss, dear. I must fly. My bath is running. Love to you both."

"Okay, Mum. Send Dad our love, too. See you Sunday."

Miranda hung up, placed the phone on the coffee table, and snuggled into Alan for a cuddle. "I knew she would be up for it. Well, that's one thing less to worry about. Has your mate got back to you about the limo yet?"

"No. I'll chase Dave up in the next day or two."

Miranda sighed. "Maybe it would have been better for everyone if we had eloped."

"And then how would we have spent our evenings?"

"Doing more making-out rather than spending masses of hours planning for one single day in our lives."

He covered her mouth with his and pulled her onto his lap. Coming up for breath, he said, "I like the making-out idea."

CHAPTER FIVE

Miranda breezed into the office the next day and regretted her buoyant mood the second Johnny waved a large wad of papers at her.

"Crap! Really? From last night's appeal?"

"Afraid so. I've made a start sifting through it, and most of it seems to be dross right now. Hopefully, it won't take long."

"Yeah, famous last words. I'll be going through the post. Give me a shout if anything interesting shows up."

Johnny nodded and renewed his examination of the papers. Miranda had her own crosses to bear in the shape of the unwanted post littering her desk. *Bang goes my bright idea of delving into Brad's background first thing.* She dipped back out of the office to buy a coffee then settled down to the least desired part of the job, despised by all of her colleagues, not just her.

Halfway through the morning, she finished the chore and joined the rest of the team in the incident room. "Anything interesting we should be chasing up?"

"I've got a few sightings of suspicious cars, ma'am. That's all," Lindsey Walker said. The bright young detective sergeant had been working alongside Miranda for a number of years, and she was meticulous when it came to organising the rest of the team.

"Can I ask you to note down all the pertinent facts of the crime on the incident board later, Lindsey? It'll be better if it's all in one place in front of our eyes."

"Sure. Let me action the CCTV footage for these possible sightings first, ma'am," Lindsey responded with a smile.

Miranda perched on the desk next to her partner and leaned forward. "Excellent. Johnny, any joy with your sifting?"

"Yes and no. I think there are a few interviews we should arrange, if that's all right?"

"Go for it. This afternoon is quite clear at present. Although I do want to start snooping into Brad's background if I have the time. This lot should take priority, however. I don't suppose anyone has reported seeing a young woman being forced into a car or building, by any chance? I know—too obvious to hope that we might get a call like that."

"Yeah, nothing like that here. Shame really. To be honest, I'm very disappointed in the response, considering a young woman is missing."

"I think the appeal is running again today, so we might still get a few more calls from it. We mustn't lose hope, Johnny. If we do that, we'll never crack the case. Okay, I'm making an executive decision and diving into Brad's personal and business background now. I'd rather visit him again once I'm armed with that knowledge."

"Yeah, I agree. There's no use going after him empty-handed in that respect. Have fun."

"I'm bound to." Miranda stepped back into her office and left the door ajar so she didn't feel cut off from her team. Something pricked her mind to ring Brad Lawrence on his mobile. *Maybe I can go ahead and make an appointment with him before I start digging.* She searched her file for his number. When the call didn't connect right away, she dialled it a second time. A foreboding niggle began to gnaw at her insides when she recognised that the tone ringing in her ear indicated that the line was no longer in use. "Johnny, come in here a minute, please?"

Within seconds, her partner ran into the office. "What is it?"

"Do me a favour? Dial this number and let me know what you get."

"Is it Lawrence's?"

Miranda nodded. He approached the desk, punched in the number, and put the phone on speaker. The detectives stared at each other, and their mouths dropped open simultaneously.

Scraping her chair on the wooden floor, Miranda stood and paced her office. "Damn, shit, blast."

"Hey, calm down, boss. Let me get on to the phone company and see if there's a problem before we start thinking the obvious."

"Okay, make it quick, Johnny. Lindsey, come in here, please?"

She appeared in the doorway. "Ma'am?"

"Leave what you're doing. I want you to get in touch with the local airports and check the airlines, see if Brad Lawrence has boarded a plane either today or yesterday evening. My inkling is that he's left the country, whilst laughing at our expense. Damn, shit, and blast!"

"Right away, ma'am."

Her two colleagues left the office. Miranda sat down and buried her head in her hands. *When are you going to trust your instincts and act upon them?*

The phone rang, interrupting her self-admonishment. She snatched it up and answered it abruptly. "Hello. DI Carr."

"Wow, sounds like someone missed out on breakfast this morning. There's no need to try and take a lump out of me to compensate for that," the chief responded jovially.

"Sorry. What can I do for you? Only I'm up to my eyes in it here."

"You sound worried. What's going on?"

"Oh nothing, except I think our main suspect has done a runner."

"Are you talking about Anneka's husband?"

"Yep. I'm so effing annoyed with myself." Miranda's anger turned to disappointment.

"Hey, you had a lot going on yesterday, what with setting up the appeal. Don't be too hard on yourself and never give up. What makes you think he's done a runner? Have you checked where he's staying?"

"No. I tried to ring him this morning on his mobile and got unobtainable. I'm just going to start trawling through his past now. Should I take a chance and visit the address he gave me?"

"Can I just clarify something first?"

"Go on." Miranda's brow creased with a frown. *Has the chief thought of something I haven't?*

"When did your police brain stop functioning?"

"I can do without the insults, chief. I'm doing my best here."

"Hey, calm down. All I'm saying is take a step back and assess all the facts you have at this time. It's not like you to jump to conclusions. You're an act-on-the-facts kind of copper, if I recall. Don't veer off that track."

"Okay, I get where you're coming from. So you think I should get all the facts sorted before I go in search of the creep?"

"Exactly. How did the appeal go? Did the information fairy visit you?"

Miranda sat back in her chair and laughed at the image the chief's words had conjured up. "Hit and miss right now. Johnny and I have a few leads to chase up this afternoon but nothing really solid. Do people walk around with their eyes closed nowadays or what?"

"Either that or they don't want the hassle of getting involved. Or it could also mean that no one genuinely saw anything. Hey, where has all this negativity come from? It's just not like you."

"Oh, I don't know. If Brad has got away, I'll be kicking myself for a long time to come. Okay, thanks for the virtual kick up the rear. If there's nothing else, I better get on. I have a suspected murderer to track down."

"You have my permission to hang up now, on one proviso."

"Which is?" Miranda asked, annoyed at the chief for playing games with her.

"Stop beating yourself up and go forth and catch the bastard!"

Miranda roared with laughter. This was why she loved Caroline being not only one of her dearest friends but also her immediate superior. She had a knack of always turning negative situations on their heads. "I will. I promise."

"Toodle pip for now," the chief signed off before she hung up.

Miranda thrust her shoulders back and booted up her computer. Within seconds, she found herself trawling the Internet for any background information she could find concerning Brad's failed business. She found it strange that the website promoting his executive travel business was still up and running. She tried to call the number on the screen, but the unobtainable tone lingered in her ear, just as it had when she'd rung his mobile a few minutes before. Refusing to be beaten, she clung to her chief's rallying words to think positive.

After an hour of searching through a combination of police programmes, she ended up with two more addresses for the couple. *But is it worth visiting the addresses?*

Breaking into her thoughts, Lindsey tapped on the door and entered the office. "Bad news, boss. I have Brad Lawrence showing up on a flight out of Gatwick first thing, bound for Portugal."

"Crap, crap, crap. Do we know when the flight landed?"

"About an hour and a half ago. And I can't see him still being at the airport after all that time."

"You're right. Okay, if he's innocent, then why has he seen fit to run?"

Lindsey nodded.

"The second question is: can we try and find out if he has a property out there?"

"Do you want me to get onto the Portuguese police, or should I go direct to Interpol?"

"Now, that's what I'm unsure about. Leave that with me for a mo. In the meantime, I'll tell you what you can do for me, Lindsey. Organise a search warrant for both these addresses." She handed the sergeant her notes.

"On it now."

Lindsey left the room, and Miranda immediately rang the chief. "Okay, chief, the shit just hit the fan."

"Meaning what? You've found Anneka's body?"

"Not yet, but we've discovered that Brad has left the country when I specifically told him not to. He flew out to Portugal first thing. Stinks of guilt to me."

"Me, too. Do you have an address in Portugal for him? Did the couple own a villa out there perhaps?"

"We're looking into that now. I wondered if you had any contacts within Interpol, or should I ring the Portuguese police first and go from there?"

"You know what? I do have a very good friend in Interpol who is based in France. I could see if he knows anyone in the Portuguese branch."

"A good friend that happens to be male, eh?"

"Yes. Hey, someday if you're nice enough to me, I might even tell you about the case that brought us together."

"Damn, no heavy romance then?"

"Hardly, although I was sorely tempted at the time. Have you ever been privy to listening to a Frenchman speak? Oh, là là!"

Miranda chuckled. "You're incorrigible. Can you get on it right away for me?"

"I'll ring him now and get back to you. Do not fret. We'll bring this guy to justice. Don't worry about that. To take off the way he has, he's definitely got something to hide."

"Thanks. I'll be waiting for your call. Damn, I just thought of something."

"What? Oh, never mind. We'll talk soon. We can share info then."

The chief hung up, and Miranda rang Anneka's parents.

"Hi, Mrs. Morton. It's DI Carr. Do you mind if I ask you a few questions over the phone, or would you prefer me to come out to the house?"

"Over the phone is fine, dear. Is it to do with the appeal? Has Anneka been seen or found?"

"Sorry to get your hopes up. No sign of Anneka yet. My team are still sifting through the information we've gained from the appeal, which, I have to tell you, is very disappointing, compared to others we have run. Sometimes, information in these cases lands on our desks a few days later, when people have had a chance to think about things more. It also went out in the local press last night, and I'm still hopeful of getting more hits from that. I'll be chasing up that side of things later—no, what I need to know from you is if either your daughter or Brad owns a property in Portugal?"

"Why, yes. Anneka bought a villa out there about four years ago. She actually uses it as a base to run the international side of her business, sort of. I mean, when she's out there, which is quite frequent, she invites all the staff running the European side of things out there for a power meeting."

"Fantastic. I don't suppose you have the address to hand, do you?"

"Just a minute." Miranda heard the phone being placed down, followed by footsteps. Sheila returned to the phone and read out the address. "It's on the Algarve, lovely part of the world, just too hot for me and James to make use of the villa in the summer months. We do go out there in the winter, but only when Anneka is staying."

"That's really helpful. While I have you on the phone, can I also take the opportunity to ask how many residences your daughter owns in the UK? Do you know offhand?"

"Of course, apart from the main house, she has two flats in London. One which she uses as a bolthole for when she's working late at the office. It's close by, you see. The other when she's entertaining prospective customers, people she is reaching out to stock her products. That one overlooks the Thames and is much swankier than the other one. Why do you ask?"

"Well, first off, we need to keep an eye on the properties, just in case the person holding your daughter turns up for some reason. You never know. Plus secondly, we can ask the neighbours if they have witnessed anything unusual going on at the addresses of late."

"I see. And that goes for the house in Portugal, too?"

"Yes, it's best if we keep an eye on all the properties. It will probably be the least likely one that comes up trumps for us in the end." Miranda hated lying to the woman, but the last thing she wanted Mr. and Mrs. Morton to do was ring the property and unintentionally alert Brad that they might know his location.

"I understand, dear. Please keep us informed, if you will?"

"Of course. You've been a great help. I'll be in touch soon. Bye for now." She hung up the phone and whooped for joy. "You're not such a smartarse, after all, are you, Bradley Lawrence?"

CHAPTER SIX

Armed with the warrants obtained from the local magistrate's court, Miranda and Johnny, accompanied by two uniformed constables, arrived at the first of Anneka's flats. After knocking on the neighbours' doors, they quickly established that no one had visited the flat for months. One of the neighbours kindly offered to ring the management company in charge of the flats to get someone to open the door rather than them using force to gain entry.

Five minutes later, the caretaker appeared and opened the door. Right away, Miranda noticed the musty smell. The neighbours had been right.

"Thank you. I appreciate your time. If either Mr. or Mrs. Lawrence visits the flat in the next few days, would you mind giving me a call?" Miranda asked the caretaker, who looked as if he were nearing retirement age.

"I'll do that for you, Inspector. No problem."

Disappointed, the four officers drove to the next location—the apartment overlooking the Thames. Again, Miranda and Johnny knocked on a few of the neighbours' doors, but everyone said the couple tended to keep to themselves. None of the neighbours were nosey enough to be bothered with what others got up to. Miranda contacted the manager of the building, who read each word on the warrant before he finally opened the door to let them in. Miranda had equipped everyone with plastic gloves. Snapping them into place, she entered the luxurious apartment. The décor and furnishings reminded her of the type she'd admired at a stately home she and Alan had visited the previous month. She didn't think the grand furniture appeared out of place in the slightest.

"Thank you. You can wait outside, if you like?" Miranda smiled at the manager.

He shook his head obstinately. "I'll stay right here until you're finished."

Miranda tilted her head. "Are you saying you don't trust the police, sir?"

"It's Mr. Ward, and no, I don't trust your lot."

Miranda thought it strange that a man whose job was to look after the wealthy inhabitants of the city should think that way. She could have understood his venomous tone if this conversation had occurred at the previous apartment, given its less luxurious surroundings, but not their current location. In the end, she decided tackling him further would serve no purpose. "Fair enough. I'm going to have to insist that you remain by the door at all times. We will be treating the flat as a crime scene. You wouldn't want your DNA spread around, would you? It could mean you spending days down at the nick for questioning."

The man's mouth hung open. Recovering, he spluttered, "No. Okay, fair enough. What sort of crime? Can I ask that?"

Miranda seemed surprised by the man's question, given the exposure the case had received in the past few days. "Have you been on holiday or something, Mr. Ward?"

"No. Why do you ask?" he replied grumpily.

"Because this case has been all over the news, both in the newspapers and on TV. Surely you must have heard that Anneka Lawrence has gone missing?"

He shook his head. "Nope. How strange. So where's her husband then?"

"We have that covered, Mr. Ward. There's no need for you to be concerned about that. Well, we must get on. Lots to do."

"Don't let me hold you up, Inspector."

Every now and again, during the course of the search, Miranda glanced in his direction to see Mr. Ward straining his ears and craning his neck to hear and see what was going on.

"Anything?" she asked the team after her own search of the couple's bedroom came up empty.

"Nothing really. Maybe we should take the address book from here? Take a gander through it ourselves rather than be told what's in it via Brad Lawrence?"

"It's a good idea, Johnny. Although things have branched off in a different direction, given the information we have gleaned since this morning." She opened her eyes wide, warning her partner not to openly discuss Brad's flight in front of the building manager.

"Okay, I understand. I'll bag it as evidence."

"Good. Maybe this is all a waste of time, and we should be thinking about moving on soon. Did you bring the list of people we need to visit?"

"The people from the appeal?" Johnny asked.

Miranda nodded.

"Yep, right here." Johnny tapped the breast pocket of his jacket. "I agree. If there's nothing major to be found here, we should move on."

"Five more minutes then, folks," Miranda announced to the rest of the team. She scanned the living room one final time before they left, but nothing further drew her attention. Maybe, just maybe, if Brad had killed his wife, it had been some kind of accident. But why would he have absconded, especially after she'd warned him not to? *Because guilty people tend to do that!*

Outside the building, Miranda ordered the uniformed officers back to the station while she and Johnny continued on to the first of the two addresses that had come their way via the appeal. The first call was to a small estate, way out in the middle of nowhere. The location alone caused Miranda to be wary of any information they might gather from the occupants of the tiny cottage. But then she chastised herself for blocking off the possibility that the location, out in the sticks, surrounded by green fields, was the ideal spot for a killer to dump or even bury a victim's body. She shuddered as she parked the car outside the house.

"What's with the shudder?" Johnny queried, looking around.

"I don't know. At first, I doubted anything would come of this enquiry, then on second thoughts, you have to imagine this being a prime spot for body-disposal purposes. Remind me what the lady saw again, before we go in?"

"A car pulled up on the common over there. Circled the area a few times. She saw a man get out, and then he drove off."

"Okay, let's see if we can jog her memory into sharing anything extra."

Miranda locked the car, and the pair of them walked up the cracked concrete path, which was bordered on either side by a variety of cottage garden plants. Miranda knocked loudly on the front door.

"Hello? What do you want?" a little voice called out from behind the locked door.

Miranda sniggered at the sound of the bolt chain being attached. "Mrs. Aston, I'm Detective Inspector Miranda Carr, and I'm here with my partner, DS Tomlin. I can push our IDs through the letterbox, if you like?"

The door inched open slightly, and Miranda held out the IDs for the woman to study. The door closed again, and Mrs. Aston removed the chain before opening the front door. She invited them through the tiny hallway into the lounge, where a roaring wood burner welcomed them.

"Hello, dears. Sorry about the security measures. You can never be too careful. It could be a mass murderer knocking, for all I know."

Miranda gave her a reassuring smile. "It's better to err on the side of caution. We're here regarding the call you made to the station about the strange goings on you witnessed on the common the other night."

"Yes, dear. Very strange, it was. I don't see many cars out here at that time of night usually, which is why I thought I'd better notify you."

"Perhaps, if you have the time, you can show us the exact spot where the incident took place. It's a pretty expansive area, after all."

"Of course. Let me get my wellies on first. Do you mind if I bring little Cherry with us? It'll save me having to take her out for a walk later."

Miranda bent down to pet the adorable pug sitting in her basket near the fire. "Will she want to leave her comfortable bed? Not a problem with me if you bring her with us. Take your time getting ready."

The old lady took Miranda at her word and didn't rush in the least. She checked and double-checked that she had everything before the three of them, plus little Cherry the dog, left the cottage. The walk was one of the slowest Miranda had ever taken, and the end result turned out to be an utter disappointment, too. They could clearly see where the car had stopped by the evidence it had left behind. The driver had discarded several black bags, which had been ripped apart by the animals venturing onto the common late at night.

"Oh!" the old lady said, screwing up her nose at the smell emanating from the sacks. "Do you think that's all he was up to? Dumping his rubbish here rather than going to the tip?"

Miranda surveyed the area and sighed deeply. "It would seem that way, Mrs. Aston. Some people really don't know how to treat our beautiful countryside well, do they?"

"Sad, very sad. I blame it on the youth and all the foreigners they're intent on letting into our country. There's disrespect everywhere you look, not that I get out much. I'm too scared to venture out most of the time. I only go out once a week to collect my pension. I go to the supermarket then, too. I clutch my bag to my chest so tight in case a young thug thinks about robbing me. It's terrible what us old folks have to put up with. And to think our brave men risked their lives back in the thirties and forties to give these animals a decent way of life. 'Shit your thanks,' as my old man used to say before he sadly departed."

"I know I shouldn't agree with you, but unfortunately I do, Mrs. Aston. Our country is changing rapidly, and to be honest with you, I'm appalled at what the general public get up to on a daily basis."

"Is it lack of money, drugs, or the alcohol to blame do you think, dear?"

"Maybe a mixture of all of them." Miranda hooked her arm through the lady's and steered her back to the cottage. They spent the next ten minutes putting the world to rights, much to Johnny's despair. Miranda shot him a warning glance every time she heard another sigh escape his lips. They finally deposited the worn-out lady at her door. Miranda threw her partner the keys while she checked around the old woman's house, adhering to her request in case any intruders had managed to strike whilst they were away. Reassured no one had entered the cottage, Miranda bid the lady farewell and climbed back in the car.

"Wow, that was a total waste of an hour," Johnny complained, banging his head against the headrest.

"It's all part of the job, man. What are you complaining about? Like Mrs. Aston pointed out, people have very little respect for people of her generation nowadays." Miranda started the car and drove off.

"Right. Let's hope we don't get landed with another old codger at the next address."

Miranda clenched her fist and punched his upper thigh. "Heartless, uncaring sod! Give the old folks a break."

"Yeah, whatever. Is there any chance of us getting something to eat today?"

Miranda looked at the clock on the dashboard. "Crap, two o'clock already. Where does the time go to?"

"That's what you get, traipsing over damp commons, steering old ladies and their dogs for an hour. It's easy to lose track of time when you're having that much fun, boss."

"Give it a rest, Johnny. Just consider it your good deed for the year, all right?"

"Make that the decade, and I'll feel happier about it."

They both laughed. However, Johnny's face clouded over the instant they pulled up outside the next property, which showed signs of being owned by a person of the same generation he'd just spent the journey complaining about.

"If you smile, I'll treat you to the largest baguette I can find at the baker's. Deal?"

He offered a smile that bordered on being more of a grimace. "Like that's going to happen. At this time of day, we'll be left with the junk all the other people have overlooked."

"Ever the optimist. You leave it to me." She winked and tapped the side of her nose.

Johnny smiled, holding up his end of the bargain. Miranda knocked on the front door of what looked to be a flat designed specifically with the older generation in mind.

A gentleman with white hair and a matching moustache opened the door. "Hello, can I help?"

The two detectives flashed their IDs, and Miranda introduced herself. "Mr. Braydon? We're here about the call you lodged with us last night."

"Ah, I see. Do you want to come in, Inspector?"

Miranda looked up at the threatening grey clouds overhead. "Looks like rain, so yes, if you don't mind."

The man pushed the door open fully, and the room he led them into was clean, though Miranda would regard it as an unloved room. No family photos adorned the walls or the sideboard, and a threadbare scatter rug covered the wooden floor.

"What else can I tell you, Inspector, other than what I've already reported?"

"If I recall correctly, you rang in and stated that you had seen a dark car driving back and forth past the house. Is that right?"

"Yes. When I said 'driving past,' I meant over a thirty-minute period, possibly longer than that. It was as though someone was looking for something, or someone maybe."

"Can you identify the car, Mr. Braydon? Did you see the number plate by any chance?"

"Sorry, not the number plate, but I recognised the car as a black Audi, one of the newer models."

"That's a great help. You said the car went back and forth. Is that going down the road?" Miranda pointed to the right.

"Yes. My guess is either the person was looking to dump something—we get a lot of fly-tipping around here what with being so close to the river, and you'd be surprised what lands up on the banks down there—or they were trying to find someone, maybe a child who hadn't returned home from school or something."

"You're very intuitive, Mr. Braydon. Can I ask you what you used to do for a living before you retired?"

"And you're very smart, Inspector. I used to be in the force. Never got any higher than constable, though. Never wanted to, either."

Miranda smiled smugly. She'd had a feeling the man had been in the police because he had that way about him. "I thought so. Okay, I wouldn't ordinarily ask a member of the public this, but given your past, I'm going to break my own rules on that. In your opinion, is it possible that the car could have been sussing the area out to possibly dump a body in the river?"

"Highly possible and even probable in my book."

"If that's the case, why didn't you say that when you rang, Mr. Braydon?"

"I had a stroke last year, Inspector, and my memory isn't what it used to be. Please forgive me. Since placing the call, I've thought of nothing else. I was awake all night, thinking things over. I'm sorry, I should have rung you back this morning. I'm fully aware of the stress involved in an appeal such as this. I didn't really want to get in your way further."

Miranda understood the man's hesitation. Since she had been a source of encouragement rather than doubt, it had given him the courage or determination to revisit the events of that night.

"It's all right, sir. I appreciate your anxiety. If there is nothing else, my partner and I would like to go now and start searching the area where you think the car went."

"Nothing else, Inspector. Although, if anything else comes to mind, I'll be sure to contact you immediately. Do you have a number I can ring?"

Miranda handed the man a business card, and they retraced their steps to the front door. "Take it easy, and get some rest. We appreciate your help."

"Let's hope you find what you're looking for down there. I wanted to go down and have a look for myself today, but time seemed to just pass me by in a flash for some reason."

"Take care, and thank you again."

"Bye-bye lunch," Johnny grumbled once they were back in the car.

"Not necessarily. Let's just take a quick scan of the area, and then we'll get back to the station to organise a proper search party."

She started the car and drove down the narrow lane. "Hmm... well, this road isn't conducive to anything other than going to or coming from a destination. Not a road I would ever think about turning into if I was wondering what was at the end of it, if you know what I'm getting at."

"Yeah, I'm sure there would be a better way of saying it than that." Johnny sniggered and focused on the road ahead.

"It made you laugh, anyway. See, stick with me, partner, and at least we'll have a bit of fun along the way. Hang on... what's this?"

Miranda pulled on the handbrake, and they both leapt out of the car. Over to the left, about ten feet from the road was a patch of long grass that had been flattened as if a vehicle had driven over it recently.

Miranda threw her arm out and grabbed Johnny's wrist before he could go any farther. "Okay, I'm thinking we should treat this like a crime scene from the outset. I've got some carrier bags in the boot. We'll slip them over our shoes."

They returned to the car, tied plastic bags around their feet, then ventured into the flattened area.

"Definitely a few tyre tracks here, as though someone parked up and reversed out in a hurry," Johnny announced, bending down to take a closer look.

"I think we've seen enough to warrant calling for backup. You sort that out while I carry on."

Johnny flipped open his mobile and called the station to speak to Craig Fulford.

Miranda moved closer and found herself stalking the area like an animal on prey alert, keeping to the very edge of the depressed area. Something that looked like the underside of a carpet or rug was partially concealed by rocks and other debris. It was roughly the same size as the one that had gone missing from the Lawrences' house. She sighed wearily. "Okay, you better make another call, Johnny."

"Don't tell me—to the pathologist?"

"Yep. I no longer think Anneka Lawrence is on the missing list."

Damn, shit, and blast!

CHAPTER SEVEN

Miranda crossed her arms and leaned against the bonnet of the car, waiting for the SOCO team and the pathologist to turn up. There was such a lot to do once a body was discovered, but the priority had to be to finding out who the victim was, and why, when and how the victim was killed. Miranda needed at least a couple of those facts before she could continue with the investigation. Then there was the horrendous task of informing the next of kin, and all this needed to be completed before the real investigation started and the hunt for the murderer began.

Pathologist Liam Gallway arrived at the scene with his entourage approximately forty minutes after Johnny placed the call. He nodded at Miranda. "Afternoon, Inspector. Let's get this tent up, boys, before the rain sets in."

"Afternoon, Liam. How's the wife?"

"Bored. Either dying to get back to work or waiting for me to retire so we can go traipsing around the world for the rest of our lives."

"You don't sound overly keen on that suggestion."

"You suspect right. The last thing I want to do is go travelling at my time of life. I'd much rather stay at home and potter around in my man shed, but no, she won't hear of that. This is her time, and she intends to enjoy it. If I've heard that once, I think I must have heard it around a million times by now."

"I'm sure you'll come to a compromise soon enough. Isn't that the recipe for a good marriage?"

"As you'll be finding out for yourself soon enough, so I hear. Good luck on that front. You'll be needing it in your line of work," he chortled and wrestled his bag from the boot of his four-by-four.

"Thanks, just what I needed to hear. Going back to the case—I don't suppose your guys have got a result for me yet, from the Lawrences' house?"

"They have, and the blood from both the tap and the bathroom floor was a positive match to the hairs on the brush. Are you thinking this is the victim?"

"Looks that way to me, Liam." Miranda fell into step beside the pathologist and approached the rolled-up carpet.

"Well, we'll see once we've run the tests, won't we?"

"I'm giving an affirmative before you carry them out. I turned back the corner—that rug, or one very similar, was reported missing from the crime scene. Call it a lucky guess, but I think that bulge in its centre will turn out to be Anneka Lawrence."

"If your *guess* is correct, then that's very sad. Apparently, money can't buy you everything. The woman was young, too, wasn't she?"

"Yes, only thirty-seven, with her whole life ahead of her. Very sad indeed."

"Let's see what we can find in the way of evidence, Inspector, so you can arrest the bastard who did this. Do you have any suspicions who that might be yet?"

"At this point, the husband seems to be the most likely suspect. He's put himself in the frame by doing a runner."

"Silly man. He's obviously never had any dealings with the intrepid Inspector Carr, the detective who seeks out, finds, and bangs up her man on a more regular basis than I can take a piss."

"Liam, that is so not true." She leaned in and whispered, "Do you have a problem in that department?"

His eyes widened. "No. I was jesting, Inspector, merely jesting with you. Why do you have to take me so literally? I thought better of you."

"Sorry, I'm off form for batting away your frivolous replies. It's been a long day, and we haven't even had lunch yet, as my dear partner has been quick to remind me."

"Ah, luncheon. What a novelty that would be for me to sit down and consume a sandwich without having the smell of the autopsy suite lingering on my clothes."

"Oh, crap. I hadn't really thought about that before. Not sure I could cope with eating amidst the smell of dried blood and rotting flesh clinging to my nostrils," Miranda replied, her mouth turning down at the sides at the thought.

"You get used to it. Right, stand back, Inspector, while the team erect the tent. Come on, boys. Let's get it rigged up before this weather turns nasty," he repeated, stressing the urgency of the situation.

"Not trying to tell you your job, Liam, but wouldn't it be better to take photos, unroll the rug, and then erect the tent? I'm remembering the size of the area the rug covered at the house, and I think if you unravel it inside the marquee, you won't be able to manoeuvre around the body freely."

Liam placed his thumb and forefinger around his chin. "Hmm... I see your point, Inspector. Okay, let's do it that way. Let's get plenty of photos first. But be quick about it."

Liam and another member of the SOCO team took what seemed like a hundred photos from different angles as the rug was unrolled. The whole process was carried out in painstaking fashion, and a full hour passed before Anneka's body was revealed.

The team worked quickly to keep out the elements threatening to spoil their examination process. The body was lifted gently onto a white sheet, and two men rolled the rug back up, placed it in a large plastic cover similar to a tarpaulin, and carried it to the van. Meanwhile, the other two members of the SOCO team erected the marquee over the body. Liam examined the body as rain pitter-pattered on the canvas overhead.

"That was close," the pathologist announced, circling the corpse, snapping shot after shot of the victim, capturing how the body had been revealed once the rug was removed. Finally, he turned the victim over and instantly glanced up at Miranda.

She stared at the corpse and nodded. "Yes, that's her. Shit, shit, shit! I'll leave you to it while I ring her parents."

Ever the practical one, Liam suggested, "I can deal with things here. Surely it would be better for you to tell the parents face-to-face. You get off and do what you have to do. I'll ring you later, let you know how we get on, all right?"

"Thanks, Liam. I appreciate it. Take good care of her. She didn't deserve this."

"No victim does, Miranda."

That's true, Miranda thought as she and Johnny trudged away from the scene. "Please don't tell me that you're still hungry after seeing that?"

"Nope. I was just going to tell you to forget about stopping off. Let's get to the Mortons' house and then back to the station. It won't hurt going without one meal for a day."

"Good man. I know I wouldn't have the stomach for it."

The Mortons' house was situated in a cul-de-sac of large detached homes. Each house was very different from its neighbour, and the façades ranged from stone to aged wood. She saw nothing too outlandish, and none of them looked at all out of place next to the other.

"Something to aim for in life, I suppose." As Miranda gazed around, a slight tinge of envy seeped through her veins.

"Nah, this all looks far too posh for my wallet. I'd rather spend my dosh on holidays and fast cars, if any should come my way in the future, that is."

"Why are men and women so different in that respect?"

Johnny shrugged and pushed open the door. "Don't you start. I get enough of that crap off Francis at home."

Miranda stood alongside him and smoothed down her jacket before she walked up the narrow path to the front door. "She's not going to put up with that two-bed starter home forever, man. You knew that from the beginning, didn't you?"

He leaned over and whispered, "Yeah, but I thought we'd be there a few years first. She's already getting itchy feet after twelve months. She has no idea how much it costs to move house, and if I raise the subject, she turns on the waterworks and tells me I don't care about her."

Miranda stifled a laugh and rang the doorbell. She cleared her throat and put on her most serious face. She heard footsteps in the hallway, then Mrs. Morton opened the door.

At first, Mrs. Morton smiled when she recognised them. However, she didn't take long to work out that the detectives were probably there to share distressing news. "James," she screeched over her shoulder.

Miranda rushed forward to help the woman as she collapsed against the wall.

Mr. Morton sprinted out of a room off the hallway and ran to his wife's aid. The colour had drained from both the Mortons' faces.

Shit! I hate this part. "Can we come inside?" Miranda asked, looking behind her to see if any of the neighbours had been alerted by the shouting.

Mr. Morton supported his wife through the house and into the large open-plan living area at the rear of the property. He walked her over to the Chesterfield leather sofa and lowered her onto it. Then he sat down heavily beside her and gestured for the detectives to sit in the matching sofa opposite. "What is it, Inspector? Have you found our daughter?"

Miranda sat down and squeezed her hands together in front of herself. She maintained eye contact with only Mr. Morton when she delivered the devastating news neither of them had wanted to hear.

"Yes, we've found your daughter. I'm sorry to have to tell you that her body was found this afternoon."

The high-pitched wail that left Mrs. Morton's mouth brought tears to Miranda's eyes, and a lump formed in her throat. Mr. Morton flung an arm around his wife's shoulders and pulled her close, burying her head against his chest. Tears flowed slowly down the couple's cheeks.

Miranda and Johnny remained quiet for the next few minutes to allow the couple's initial grief to flow. After that, Miranda spoke. "I'm so sorry for your loss. I'm not trying to make excuses for our part in not finding Anneka sooner, but the specialists felt after encountering the blood at the scene, that Anneka was probably dead before her body was removed from the house. I didn't say anything at the time because I didn't want to give you any misinformation."

"No! Instead, you left us with a sense of hope that she might be returned to us intact. Why would you do that, Inspector?" Mr. Morton asked in a choked voice.

"I'm sorry if it came across that way, Mr. Morton. I can assure you that wasn't my intention at all. In cases such as this, it is very difficult for the investigating officers to know what to do for the best. If I'd told you that I thought there was no way your daughter could have survived such an attack, she might have ended up walking through the door a few days later, and I would have been in the wrong then, too."

"I appreciate that, Inspector. Although, *we* would have rather heard that than been given the false hope of her return."

Miranda's guilt intensified under the man's glare. "I'm sorry for the added pain I have caused in that case."

"Accepted," Mr. Morton replied.

"You're not being fair, James. The inspector's job could never be described as being an easy one. It's not her fault someone killed our beautiful daughter, and it is not going to help if we fall out with the investigating officer, is it?" Turning to Miranda, she wiped her nose with the edge of a tissue and added, "I'm sorry, Inspector. The news has come as a shock to both of us."

"No need to apologise, Mrs. Morton."

Her breath was wracked with sobs. "Can I ask how the appeal went? Is this how you discovered... Anneka?"

"Yes, we had two calls pointing out two different events. We followed up on both of them as soon as we could, and the second call, from an ex-copper, turned out to be very significant indeed." Miranda paused, wondering whether she should divulge what she knew about Brad or whether she should leave it a few days until she had more concrete evidence to share with the grieving couple. Given Mr. Morton's earlier reaction, she decided to tell them a snippet of what she had learned. "There is one thing I'd like to share with you."

The couple glanced at each other, wearing puzzled expressions. "What's that?" Mr. Morton asked.

"We think Brad is behind your daughter's death, either directly or indirectly. We're not sure yet."

"What? Why?" asked Mrs. Morton.

"We've yet to find out the reason why. Look, let's leave this here today. You need to grieve before I start bombarding you with questions. We know where he is."

"Where?" the couple enquired in unison.

"He boarded a plane first thing this morning and headed out to Portugal."

"That's why you wanted to know if Anneka owned any property out there," Mrs. Morton said, nodding.

Miranda raised her hand in front of her. "Look, I know how tempted you will be to contact him or go out there in person, but please, I'm begging you to restrain yourselves. Leave that side of things for me to sort out. My DCI is already contacting Interpol to see where we stand there. He'll be extradited if the need arises, I assure you. Please, just concentrate on saying goodbye to Anneka. Don't let him absconding deter you from grieving properly."

"I'm not comfortable about him being out there on the loose, Inspector, but I will abide by your wishes, for now," Mr. Morton said.

Miranda sensed that if she didn't draw the case to a rapid conclusion, Anneka's father would not hesitate to exact revenge on his son-in-law, once Anneka's funeral was out of the way.

"Another thing. Is the launch still going ahead? I think it should. It would go a long way to show the world, and Brad, that nothing will stand in the way of Anneka's excellent work forging ahead in spite of her death. Jessica seems more than capable of taking over and seeing the launch through to the end, from what I've seen of her anyway."

"We've discussed this numerous times since yesterday and have decided that I should give Jess a hand at least in the interim period," Mrs. Morton said." Like you say, it would be a shame to throw in the towel now and let Anneka's hard work go to waste. Jess and I can work together for the next few months until I can appoint someone else. I'm sure there will be plenty of applicants for the role." Mrs. Morton sat upright showing what a determined lady she could be given the circumstances she was forced to deal with.

"That makes sense and will help occupy your mind. I don't mean that disrespectfully, just that if you have time to dwell on your daughter's death, you might set out and do something you later regret." She smiled at Mr. Morton, hoping that he would see through her message and understand that she had voiced the statement for his benefit.

"We understand totally, Inspector. James, will you organise the funeral while I get on with the launch? Let's stick two fingers up to Brad, and to the rest of the cosmetic world for that matter, and make this launch the best the industry has ever seen. What a wonderful legacy that would be for our daughter."

Mr. Morton pecked his wife on the cheek. "I'll take it on, dear, on the proviso that you don't work yourself into the ground for this damned launch. That's why you handed over the reins to Anneka in the first place, remember? Things have a habit of getting on top of you quickly, and you end up working seventeen- or even eighteen-hour days to compensate. I'll not let you do that to yourself again, Sheila, given your health issues."

His wife ran a hand down his cheek. "Just bear with me for a week. At the end of that time, we'll both need a break. Maybe we can think of somewhere beautiful we can visit to scatter Anneka's ashes."

"That sounds like an excellent idea, Mrs. Morton. I'll be sure to have a word with the pathologist to let him know your intentions." Miranda smiled, nudged Johnny with her elbow, and stood up. "Right, we'd better go now. Again, you have my number. Don't hesitate to ring me if you need any questions answered or vice versa if you discover anything further I should know."

The Mortons both stood, shook hands with Miranda and Johnny, then saw them to the front door.

In the car, Johnny was quick to point out, "Wow, they took that well. I don't think I've witnessed a grieving couple respond like that before."

"It's surprising what determination does to a person, partner. And I can tell the Mortons are two very determined people. Let's just say, I'm going to do everything in my power to make sure they remain on our side in this."

"Do you have any doubts about that, boss?"

Miranda started the engine and turned to look at him. "I think if Brad isn't caught quickly, there's every chance that Mr. Morton will fly out to Portugal to issue his own form of justice."

"We better catch Brad first to ensure that doesn't happen then. Otherwise, Mrs. Morton might be holding two funerals soon, instead of only one."

The minute she and Johnny arrived back at the station, Miranda called the team together to share the sad news. "Okay, guys, listen up. One of the calls we received from the appeal turned out to be valuable information, which just goes to show why we must always follow up on leads, no matter how insignificant that might seem in the first instance. The caller, an ex-copper, by the way, pointed out an area close to his home in which he'd seen a car acting suspiciously. When we tracked down the location, we discovered Anneka Lawrence's body."

Groans of anguish filled the room.

"Did the witness confirm who was driving the car, ma'am?" Lindsey asked, tapping a pen against her chin.

"No, but I'm guessing if we locate Brad Lawrence's car, there will be significant evidence in the boot corroborating our theory that he murdered his wife."

"Do you want me to put a call out for uniform to search the Gatwick Airport car park?"

"Yep, I was just about to suggest the same, Lindsey. Get on to that straight away, if you will."

"I'm on it." She reached for the phone while Miranda carried on with the meeting.

"So what's happening about Brad? Is someone going out there to haul his arse back here, or what?" asked Joseph Morgan, one of the older members of the team, who lacked any ambition to climb the promotional ladder.

"I'm just going to try and organise something along those lines now. First, I need to know if you guys have come up with anything since we've been out."

Joseph and Craig shook their heads.

"No, ma'am. You and Johnny followed up anything that even remotely looked as if it had legs from this appeal. Not that it matters a jot now that we've found the body," Craig said.

"Okay, let's stick with it. Johnny, keep looking into Brad's background, go further afield, take a look through the Portuguese archives, will you?"

"All right. Anything and everything, yes?"

"You've got it. I'll be with the DCI if you need me." Miranda walked along the corridor and tapped on an office door.

Cindy Jackman, the DCI's secretary, welcomed her in.

"Hi, Cindy. Any chance of a quick word with the chief?"

"Sure, Miranda. She always has time for you." She glanced at the phone on her desk. "She's finished her call. Go right in."

"Thanks. I hope she doesn't bite my head off for the intrusion."

"Not at all. I think she has some good news for you."

"Thanks, I could do with a dose of that." Miranda knocked and entered the room when the chief called out. "Hi, you wanted to see me?"

The chief tilted her head. "No. Who gave you that idea?" she asked suspiciously.

"Okay, I'll hold my hands up. I have news for you, but Cindy hinted that you might have news for me in return. Do you want to go first, or shall I?"

The chief placed a finger in the air and motioned for Miranda to be patient, then pressed the intercom on her desk. "Cindy, can you rustle up two white coffees with sugar please?"

"Yes, ma'am," Cindy responded.

"You first?" Caroline asked.

Miranda sat opposite and folded her arms. "We've found Anneka Lawrence's body. The pathologist is on the scene now."

"Shit! Where was she?"

"Down by the river. Thank God an ex-copper called in a suspicious sighting of a car. I fear it would've been days before the body was discovered otherwise. It's a pretty remote area, and the road was a kind of dead end, very narrow anyway."

"I take it you've informed the parents?" the chief asked.

Cindy brought in the coffee, and Miranda delayed answering until the secretary left the room again.

"Yeah, Johnny and I have just come from there."

"Silly question, but are they all right? Do they know who the main suspect is?"

"They were upset. Mrs. Morton is more determined than ever to complete the launch, though. In the meantime, Mr. Morton will carry out the funeral arrangements."

"Poor people. It really couldn't have occurred at a worse time for them."

"I think there are fors and againsts for this situation. On the one hand, they'll be devastated that Anneka isn't around to share in the success, and on the other, they'll be too distracted with ensuring the launch goes well that it'll probably help them get over the grieving process quicker. Harsh thing to say, but I bet I'm right."

"Sad, that she had to die and not see all her hard work come to fruition. Heartless piece of shit her husband must be. I can't believe you didn't pick up on that when you were in the same room as him."

Miranda took a sip of coffee, thinking it would stop her from grinding her teeth at the chief's observation. "Hey, I feel guilty enough about letting the fucker go as it is without you getting on my back and taking pleasure pointing out the bloody obvious."

"Oops, you know I wasn't blaming you. Anyway, I need to share my news with you now."

"Go on. You have a twinkle in your eye that I know is going to get one of us in trouble. Bear in mind that I've had my share of crap to contend with today." Miranda gave her boss a brief smile and waited impatiently for Caroline to share the news. The chief always tended to play up her part and took pleasure in seeing other people panting like eager puppies. Miranda had seen through her boss's shenanigans from the very beginning and did everything she could not to rise to the bait.

"You're such a spoilsport at times."

Miranda nodded, disappointing her boss even more.

"All right. I've been in touch with my man friend at Interpol, and they've managed to track down Brad Lawrence."

Miranda sat forward in her chair. "Wow, how fantastic. Was he at the house? They've arrested him, yes?"

"No. I told them not to arrest him."

Miranda frowned. "What? Why? Why would you do that and risk him taking off again?"

"One simple reason." Caroline took a sip from her cup to prolong the pause.

"Christ, Caroline, spit it out, will you?"

"You're forgetting one major fact about the crime."

"I am?"

"Yes. You told me that Anneka's body was wrapped in a heavy rug, which led you to assume that Brad had an accomplice. Am I right?"

"Shit! Yes, of course. So, what do you suggest we do now?"

"Hop on a plane."

Miranda's mouth hung open, and she stared at the grin developing on the chief's face. Recovering, she asked, "You mean go out there?"

"Yep. We could have a girlie break at the Met's expense."

Miranda's eyes bulged. "What? You and me go out there? Are you bloody mad?"

"It has been said many a time, dear friend. Is your passport up to date?"

"Of course it is. Jesus, I can't just take off like that."

It was Caroline's turn to frown. "Why on earth not? What's stopping you? I know Alan wouldn't do such a thing?"

"No, you're right there. Oh, shit! I don't *know*. The whole idea has caught me off guard."

"Off guard is okay. I've booked us on a flight first thing in the morning."

"Bloody hell. Give a girl a chance to pack her bags, will you?"

"No bags. Not the kind you're thinking about. Shove everything in a holdall and be done with it. We'll be there and back before you can learn how to say 'Mine's a sangria' in Portuguese."

"You're crazy, woman. I think you'll find that sangria is a Spanish drink not Portuguese."

"What do they drink then?"

"How the heck should I know! Crap, any chance I can knock off early tonight?"

"Nope! If I have to put in a bloody full day, then you're going to have to do the same, matey."

"And there was me telling Johnny only the other day what a kind, caring boss and friend you were. I guess I'll have to admit to him that I lied about those wonderful attributes."

"Get out of here. I'll let you knock off an hour early. Make sure your team work their butts off while you're out of the country. You hear me? I don't want to come back and have to start handing out warnings left and right for shoddy work."

Miranda finished her coffee and stood up to leave. "Do you want me to drop by and pick you up in the morning, or will you make your own way there?"

"Would you mind? It seems silly to take two cars. The flight is at seven. We need to check in an hour before, so we better get on the road by five thirty, agreed?"

"Crap! Couldn't you have booked a later flight? That means I'll have to get up at four thirty."

"Nonsense. There's no need for you to have a shower or put on your war paint."

"Piss off. I ain't going anywhere without jumping in the shower first. I have some pride left, even if you don't."

Miranda ran from the room, narrowly avoiding the book the chief aimed at her head. Cindy laughed when she heard it clatter against the door.

"She loves me, really. You can tell that, right?"

CHAPTER EIGHT

Even after a cold shower the next morning, Miranda wasn't fully awake. *Crap! It's still dark out here.* She'd recently been diagnosed with night blindness at the optician's, so she reached into her glove compartment for the new specs she'd picked up only last week. They had remained locked away ever since her appointment. She blew out a long shuddering breath and secured them into position. The instant she took her hand away, the frames felt heavy enough to make her think they were made of lead, and they dug into the sides of her nose.

Jesus, how the hell do people wear these things twenty-four-seven? By the time she arrived at Caroline's house ten minutes later, her eyes felt red raw, and her nose twitched as though she was about to have a sneezing fit. Caroline's shocked face did nothing to ease her discomfort, either. "Don't you dare!" she warned her boss.

Caroline jumped into the passenger seat. "What? I was only going to say good morning. I was considering adding 'four eyes' at the end but thought better of it."

"Good. I'm glad you saw sense before I had to knock it into you," Miranda retorted.

"Oh my, we did get out of the wrong side of bed this morning, didn't we, Inspector?" Caroline taunted her light-heartedly.

"No, I didn't. The fact that I haven't slept a bloody wink all night and then I have to be seen in these shitty things might have something to do with my less-than-cheerful mood."

"Ah, okay. Shall I take that as a warning and keep my mouth shut for the duration of the trip?"

"Just let me get to the airport in one piece while suffering in silence. Don't get the hump with me like you usually do."

Caroline laughed and tickled Miranda under the chin. "Diddums, you stay quiet and sulk while I sort out the plan for when we land all by myself."

"Shut up. Let me concentrate, and we'll discuss any plans we need to put into action at the airport. Stop trying to wind me up, lady."

"Not me. Totally innocent on that front. I can't help it if you're a tad oversensitive right now. My advice would be to have a word with that fiancé of yours, tell him not to ravish you every night if this is the result."

Miranda glared at her boss but said nothing.

They made it to the airport with ten minutes to spare. In the departure lounge, they ordered coffee and ran through their action plan.

"I've been informed that a Sergeant Tiago Lisboa will meet us at Faro Airport. Let's hope he's fit." Caroline nudged Miranda and winked.

Miranda shook her head in despair. "You're terrible. I hope this isn't going to be one big joke to you when we get out there. We haven't got time for flirting and setting up dinner dates with our foreign counterparts."

Caroline wrinkled her nose. "Spoilsport. *You* might not be single, but I'm not..."

"Yeah, I know. Go on, I'll even finish the sentence off for you. 'But I'm not getting any younger. So if opportunity comes knocking, I should welcome it with open arms.' Did I leave anything out?"

Caroline giggled. "No. Christ, you do know me well. All right, I promise to behave myself, only if he turns out to be butt ugly, though. Deal?"

Miranda's hands remained firmly clasped around her cup. "You call that a deal?"

"It's the best you're likely to get from me. No, in all seriousness, you've obviously lost your sense of humour since slipping on those glasses of yours. We're here to do a job. Let's see if we can get Brad hauled back home within two days. How does that sound?"

"Like an eternity. Not sure I can handle spending forty-eight hours in your bloody company."

"Charming! Is that any way to speak to your superior?"

"You forgot the 'dear friend' part."

"Yeah, how could I forget that?"

At that moment, their flight number was announced. After picking up their overnight bags, they followed the small crowd through to the departure gate. Miranda's stomach started its usual churning once she saw the plane waiting at the gate. Her most recent flight had been to Florida, and she and Alan had wound up in a bout of turbulence, during which the plane had dropped several hundred feet. She regretted neglecting to tell her boss that when the subject of jumping on a plane to Portugal had cropped up.

"Are you all right? You've gone deathly white."

Miranda tried but failed to give Caroline a reassuring smile. "I'll be better once we're in Portugal."

"Oh, crap! Why didn't you tell me you were scared of flying? You and Alan used to travel abroad a lot, I seem to recall. Don't tell me you travelled everywhere by boat?"

"No, of course not. A dodgy flight put paid to our excursions a few years ago. This is the first time I've flown since we nearly dropped out of the sky."

Caroline tutted. "Jesus, woman. You've got a bloody tongue in your head. Why in God's name didn't you tell me?"

"Like I had a choice. I'll be fine. Don't fret about me."

"Well, to me, you look anything but bloody fine. Shall I see if they've got some kind of sedative to knock you out?"

She laughed despite the severity of the problem. "They wouldn't do that, you idiot. Stop worrying."

Miranda and Caroline showed their passports to the check-in attendant and passed through without a hitch. When the plane was finally loaded and the engines roared into life, Miranda clutched her boss's hand and continued to do so for the remainder of the take-off.

Once the plane had levelled out after its vertical climb, Caroline tapped the back of Miranda's hand. "You can let go now. Or are you intending to cut off my circulation for the rest of the flight?"

"I wonder if it's too early to get a drink?" Miranda joked, although something to settle her nerves certainly sounded like a good idea.

"May I remind you that you're on duty, Inspector?"

"You can remind me all you like—it won't stop me craving alcohol." Miranda threw her head back against the headrest.

"Read an in-flight magazine or watch a video to distract you."

"I'm going to try and catch up on the sleep I missed out on last night, if you don't mind."

"Go for it. I'll nudge you when we're about to land."

Miranda turned to look at her. "After would be preferable."

The flight went without the unexpected hitches, and they were met by a short, dumpy man in the arrival lounge. He held up a piece of cardboard. Written on it in thick black marker was Caroline's name.

"That's me." Caroline shook the man's hand and introduced them both. "Do you speak English?"

"Of course. There is a car waiting outside to take you to the police station."

"And you are?"

"I'm sorry, I forgot to introduce myself. I will be your contact while you are here in Portugal. Tiago Lisboa. We will talk more at the station. Let's get out of here before the traffic defeats us."

They jumped in the back of the car awaiting their arrival. The sun's rays filled the car, forcing both women to remove their jackets and open the rear window to gain some air.

"Have you managed to locate Brad Lawrence yet, Tiago?" Miranda asked, peering out at the slow-moving traffic, feeling claustrophobic.

"I said we will discuss it at the station."

And that was the sum total of conversation that took place during the half-hour journey. Infuriated by the man's unwillingness to divulge what he knew about the suspect, Miranda spent most of the trip sighing and thinking up questions to bombard the sergeant with once they reached their destination. She had an inkling that Caroline was doing the very same thing by the way her hands were clenching and unclenching in her lap.

The car pulled up outside the station, and a uniformed policeman arrived within seconds to unload their bags for them.

"We'll keep these in a safe room for now until you are ready to go to your hotel. Come with me." Tiago marched ahead down a few winding, whitewashed corridors to a room filled with computers and a group of five men. "This is our command centre, if you like. All talk about this investigation should take place in this room and nowhere else. Is that clear, ladies?"

Miranda and Caroline gave each other a puzzled look. "May I ask why? Do you not trust the local police, Tiago?" Caroline queried.

"It's the way it has to be. The fewer people who know about this investigation, the better. Don't you agree? Do you not work on the same principles in the Metropolitan Police Force?"

Miranda couldn't dispute that point. "I suppose so. Can we get down to business now? My colleague asked you a question in the car which requires an answer."

"Ah, yes. Forgive me. Again, I did not want to discuss the investigation in the car with an outsider, with the driver present. It's not good practice to have wagging tongues. Do you agree?"

"Yes, you made your opinion perfectly clear. If we can get on now? Is Brad Lawrence in the area, Sergeant?"

"Yes, he is at the villa he shares with his wife."

Miranda cringed. "Okay, I think we need to bring you up to speed on what has transpired regarding the case. Yesterday, we discovered Anneka's body. So this is now an official murder enquiry, and Mr. Lawrence is our prime suspect."

Tiago rested his backside on one of the desks and placed his hands on his thighs. "That is very unfortunate. So are you looking to get Mr. Lawrence extradited? That will take several days to arrange."

"That was the plan, yes. Is there any way we can hurry things along? We had hoped our trip would be a short one—the shorter, the better, in fact," Caroline said to the sergeant.

"These things take time to sort out, ladies. In the meantime, we intend to keep Mr. Lawrence under tight surveillance. You, on the other hand, should take the opportunity to enjoy our beautiful country and this wonderful weather. It looks like you could both do with exposing your skin to a little of our sunshine."

Miranda glanced sideways at Caroline, aware of how much the man's patronising words would be riling her boss, then Miranda corrected him. "We're not here to sun ourselves, Tiago. Let's get that clear from the off, okay? Now, if you don't mind, the Inspector and I would like a cup of coffee and to be brought up to date on what you have discovered so far about Mr. Lawrence and his activities since his arrival here yesterday?"

A smirk appeared on the sergeant's face then quickly dissipated. Miranda got the impression he wasn't used to a woman speaking to him in such an authoritative manner or tone. He stood up and crossed the room. He stopped at a desk at the rear and picked up a folder stuffed with paper. Returning, he placed the folder on the desk he'd just vacated and tapped the top of it with his chubby little hand. "Here is all the information we have managed to collate so far on the suspect."

Caroline stepped forward and flipped open the file's cover. "Helpful." She closed it again and walked back to stand beside Miranda. "It's all in Portuguese."

Miranda snorted. "Don't tell me you expected it to be in English, Caroline?"

"I hoped it would be," she stated out of the corner of her mouth.

"Let me sort out some drinks for us all, then I will run through the documents and give you a brief synopsis."

"Thank you. We'd appreciate that, Tiago." Caroline smiled openly at the man.

The sergeant left the room. Miranda shuffled closer to Caroline and whispered, "Do you really think he's going to tell us all they've found in those files?"

"Why shouldn't he? Aren't we working on the same side? You're too mistrusting. That's your problem, Miranda."

Her eyes widened in shock. "Really? Is that what you really think of me?"

"It was a joke. Lighten up, will you? Let's play it cool with the locals, yes? You start getting his back up, giving him smart remarks, and he's likely to stop sharing before he even begins. You need to be crafty with these guys."

"We'll see."

Tiago returned, carrying a tray holding a number of mugs, which impressed Miranda. Not everyone in his rank back in the UK would consider supplying everybody in the room with a mug of coffee whilst getting his own. *Maybe he's not so bad, after all.*

"Help yourselves. Sugar is in short supply at the station, sorry. Let's start, shall we?" He opened the file as both women reached for a mug of coffee and reluctantly sipped at it. "Right, he arrived at his home yesterday around midday, I believe. So far, he hasn't left the villa or received any guests."

"Okay. You say you've delved into his background. Can you tell us what you've uncovered there?" Caroline asked.

"I suspect along the same things you have ascertained yourselves. He used to run an exclusive travel company, which went bankrupt. Is that what you found out, too?"

"Yes. I don't suppose you've had a chance to speak to the neighbours at all?" Miranda asked. She took out her notebook.

"Why would we involve the neighbours in our enquiries? It is better to keep quiet about this, isn't it?"

"Yes, at the moment, I agree. I just wondered if they might have been able to shed any light on what sort of activities went on at the house. For all we know, Lawrence could be some kind of drug baron."

He tilted his head back and let out a full belly laugh that set off the rest of his colleagues, too. Miranda's cheeks reddened quickly.

"It's true, men. They say the British police have vivid imaginations."

Luckily, Caroline came to Miranda's rescue. "It was a simple enough observation, Tiago. There is no need to ridicule the inspector for the way she phrased her point of view. So, are you telling us that Portugal is squeaky clean and that it has no history of drug trafficking in the slightest?"

Tiago nodded briefly. "I apologise. Forgive my rudeness, Inspector. No, I'm not saying that at all. I just wouldn't associate that particular crime with this suspect."

"As opposed to murder, you mean?" Caroline was quick to counter.

He smiled tautly. "Ah, I understand what you are saying. It was foolish of me to laugh at the inspector, given the facts you have already gathered."

After Caroline's dressing down, the sergeant appeared to respect and appreciate both the women's perspectives on Brad's behaviour and what he was likely to do next. After finding only the usual problems in the suspect's past, everyone agreed that the two female detectives should check into their hotel to clean up and rest for a few hours before beginning their surveillance of the suspect, whilst awaiting the extradition order to be actioned.

"What do you make of things?" Miranda asked, letting them both into the small but adequate hotel room furnished with a double bed.

"The bed? I think it's too bad there aren't two singles or a couch one of us could take."

"I wasn't referring to that. I'll sleep on the floor. It doesn't bother me."

"You will not. But if one word gets back to the rest of the team that we shared a bed, I'll issue immediate orders for your demotion."

Miranda stared at her boss. "Yeah, right. Fond of cutting your nose off, aren't you? I was asking what you make of our new friend, Tiago?"

"Ah, well, I think he'll conform nicely now that we've shown him who's in charge of the case. He can pull the territory shit if he wants, but we all know he was speaking out against the fact that we're both women stepping on his toes, or trying to. He should know better than to do that with either of us. I don't think he'll be tempted to do that sort of thing a second time."

"I know he slapped me down about asking the neighbours, but I still think it's worth a shot. We could pretend to be tourists on the lookout for a property in the area or something like that. What do you think?"

"I think we should take the opportunity to rest for a while and then reconsider what we do next. You might be right about the neighbour's angle, though."

"Okay, I bow to your better judgement. I want to ring the station first to check how things are progressing there. Can I use the hotel phone rather than my mobile?"

"Go for it."

Miranda dropped onto the edge of the bed and picked up the phone. "Do you think I dial direct or would I need to go through the receptionist?"

"You should be able to dial direct."

Miranda rang the number and asked the control room operator to put her through to her partner.

"Hello. DS Tomlin speaking."

"Johnny, it's me. How are things going back at the ranch?"

"Good morning, boss. Well, while you and the chief have been sunning yourselves, we've been working our socks off."

"Yeah, yeah. Go on, what have you found?" Miranda gave the thumbs-up signal to Caroline, who was busy unpacking the few clothes she had brought.

"Well, we've located Lawrence's car at Gatwick. It's on its way into forensics now."

"That's excellent news, Johnny. Well done, you. Any other information come in from the appeal, or have the phones died down on that front?"

"Nothing there. Not sure anyone could add anything more than what we know already, boss. Dare I ask how things are going out there? Are the natives obliging?"

She laughed. "That's debatable at present. At the moment, we have very little to report; only that Brad is at the villa. We're starting the surveillance on the house this afternoon. So we'll know more later, I suspect. The extradition order has been actioned. As soon as that is signed off, it'll be all systems go and time to hop on a plane back to London. You'll be pleased to know that the weather is beautiful. Unfortunately, I won't have time to send you all a postcard."

"That's a shame. I hope the chief is behaving herself?"

"She is. Right, I better go now. Listen, if you need me urgently, send me a text. We'll be out in the field most of the time. I'll get back to you as soon as I possibly can, all right?"

"Yep. Okay, have fun."

She hung up. "Good news, they've found Lawrence's car."

"That's great news. Looks like everything is going our way. Not many cases where that can be said, eh?"

"I was thinking the same thing. Everything is running too smoothly, though, if you ask me."

"Miranda, Miranda, ever the pessimist—even when the evidence and the suspect is within touching distance."

"Yeah, but he's not within our grasp yet, is he? Until we've accomplished that, I'm always going to have a niggling doubt in my abdomen."

"If your doubt monitor is running that high, maybe that's reason enough to work out a plan B for trapping the bastard. What do you think?"

"I'm all for thinking outside the box. You know that. I don't see what harm it can do. Any chance we can catch a few hours kip first? I'm exhausted."

"What? Didn't you sleep enough on the plane? Never mind. You carry on. I'll take my notebook downstairs and sit by the pool for a few hours, see what I can come up with."

"Crap, now you're making me feel guilty. Would it be so bad if I decided to tag along and doze in the sun instead?"

Caroline laughed. "Do what you like. No one says that you have to lie in here and rest. Did you bring a swimsuit?"

"No. I didn't think to pack one. Hey, I don't want to get scorched. Will shorts and a T-shirt suffice?"

"That's the route I'm going down. You've got five minutes to get changed. Maybe we can pick up a bikini or something in that little shop we passed downstairs in the reception area."

The shop was virtually empty, no use at all to anyone staying in the hotel. They arrived at the hotel pool to find their only source of company was in the form of the numerous varieties of palm trees scattered around the pool, offering sunbathers the chance to stretch out in a little shade when the heat became unbearable. The pool looked inviting, and Miranda mentally kicked herself for not thinking to bring her bikini with her. The thought hadn't even crossed her mind. She hadn't expected to be sunbathing instead of arresting the suspect and hauling his arse back to the UK. *Bloody paperwork—it's the bane of my effing life.*

"Well, this is the life. Sunbathing in the heat of a Mediterranean sun, notebook in hand, running through police business. Hey, maybe we should consider leaving the Met and go down the Interpol route. We'd certainly get some colour on our skin for a change."

"I doubt if either of us could cope with the heat. Sure, the first few months would be a novelty, but that would surely wear off after a while. It's all right for you being single. Some of us have family members to consider when making life changing decisions like that."

"God, Miranda, lighten up. I was only joking."

"Sorry. Put it down to the stress of the wedding. You know I'm not usually so black and white about things."

They both sat on the edge of two sun loungers, and Caroline reached over to grasp Miranda's hand. "You know you can talk to me anytime, don't you?"

"Yeah, I know. It's just a heavy weight I have to bear at the moment, on top of the fire at my parents' business. Roll on September—that's all I can say."

"You'll look back on this time with a smile and say to yourself that all the angst was worth it once you have Alan as your hubbie, love."

"Yeah, probably. I wanted to ask your advice about changing my name. Do you think I should stick with Carr or change it to Rogers after the wedding?"

Caroline shrugged. "If you're only intending on getting married once, then I would say change it. If on the other hand, you're going to turn out to be a serial marriager like me, then I'd plump for remaining Carr. Less confusion that way."

Miranda chuckled. "Is there such a term as *serial marriager*?"

"There is in my personal dictionary. I'm living proof of it. Right, you take a snooze while I jot a plan that's brewing down. Chill, baby girl."

Surprisingly, Miranda didn't take long to drop off to sleep. Even her dream was littered with wedding angst, which meant that she woke up within half an hour, feeling far worse than she had before drifting off in the first place. She sat up and glanced around, trying to get her bearings. "Crap, that didn't go according to plan. Fancy a drink?"

"A cold one, please. If you get those, I'll put the finishing touches to this and then run through it with you."

Miranda headed into the bar and ordered two non-alcoholic cocktails. The barman offered her a sexy smile, which didn't interest her in the least. He was far too pretty for her tastes, even if she hadn't been a betrothed woman. She thanked him and returned to where Caroline was reclining, her eyes closed against the sun's increasing heat. "Here you go."

"What's this? I hope it's laced with vodka?"

"Fat chance. Come on then, I'm dying to hear what you have in mind."

Caroline sipped her drink through the straw and placed her tall glass on the table beside her. "Okay, this is about having a plan B to hand, remember? Not something we should be looking at jumping ahead with from the word *go*. Is that clear? You know what Tiago was saying about Lawrence liking the ladies?"

Miranda nodded and narrowed her eyes.

"Well, I think I should set myself up as a target for him. Pretend I'm wealthy and looking for *luuurve*."

"That simple, eh? Aren't you forgetting something?"

"Such as?" Caroline asked, her brow furrowing.

"The clothes you brought with you hardly broadcast you're a wealthy heiress of whatever you intend posing as."

"Yeah, I've already thought about that. I always like to do a little shopping when abroad. Do you think I'd get away with putting it on expenses?"

"Nope. The super would have instant heart failure if you did that."

"That's a minor problem to overcome anyway. With what the sergeant said about him having a wandering eye, do you think he's likely to take the bait?"

"Not only the sergeant, Anneka's PA said something along those lines, too. The question is, could you cope with him mauling you? I know I couldn't. The thought of those hands, the same hands that killed his wife, touching my skin would have me reaching for the first sharp object I could lay my hands on." Miranda shuddered at the image of Brad touching her.

"I'd have to blank out that side of things, of course. You've done undercover work before. You know the drill."

Miranda inhaled and exhaled a noisy breath. "And this is definitely a plan B only? Not something you're going to entertain soon."

"It could be soon, but yes, let's see how things pan out first. Do you think I could pull it off?"

"To be honest, no. Remove those bloody daggers from your eyes. You're too rusty for this type of shit. I think if anyone goes undercover, it should be me."

"Christ, Alan would have my tits served up for supper if I put you in the frame for this job. No, it's my plan—I should be the one who puts herself in danger. Anyway, you're forgetting one major fact."

"Which is?"

"Brad knows you."

Miranda pulled a face at her friend. "In that case, we have a lot of intricate details we need to go through first in order to keep you safe. Are you proposing going in the villa?"

"Of course." Caroline took another long sip from her drink.

"Then we need to get some sort of design plan of the house. I refuse to let you enter that place not knowing if he has a secret area where he could stash you or even torture you."

Caroline's eyes almost popped out of her head at the suggestion.

"Don't look so shocked, Caroline—we're talking about trying to trap a man who is probably filled with adrenaline after just successfully murdering his wife, for fuck's sake. You really haven't thought this through enough if you think all he's going to do is wine and dine you and say good night. These types of bastards never do things that way."

"All right, smartarse. That's what we're trying to figure out now, isn't it? Geez… give a chief inspector a break now and again."

Miranda shook her head and smiled. "It was just a ploy to get my input, wasn't it? Go on, be honest. You're so rusty, the cogs in that little brain of yours are grinding to a halt."

Caroline threw the notebook on the bottom of the recliner and stretched out in the sun. "If you can do better, I suggest you get on with it."

Miranda knew that Caroline was only joking. She was also aware of her good friend's intentions to get her involved ensuring her mind was off the distractions of the wedding. "As per usual, leave me to pick up all the pieces. Right, where were we before you pulled a boss's strop?" Miranda picked up the notebook and scanned Caroline's notes. Surprisingly, her friend had filled several pages. However, most of the ideas were riddled with flaws. Miranda laughed.

Caroline lifted her sunglasses into her hairline and glared at her. "What's so funny?"

"You. Or should I say your ludicrous ideas?"

"Such as what?"

"A number of basic errors in your planning proves to me that I should be the one going in undercover, not *you*." To be honest, most of the flaws in Caroline's plans were minor, but Miranda wasn't about to give in and let her chief off lightly. If there was a chance of her getting in that villa instead of Caroline, she was about to grab it with both hands.

"We've already covered this. He knows you, you idiot."

Miranda tutted and tilted her head. "Doh, I would be in disguise. That would be the natural thing to do, wouldn't it?"

"No way. Seriously, if the guy is that devious, he'd cotton on to you within a few seconds."

"Really? Maybe if we were back in the UK, but would he really be expecting to be fooled by a British copper out here?"

Caroline twisted in her recliner and placed her feet on the ground. "It would make sense for you to go in there. You're far more devious than I am, anyway."

"Ha! Thanks. I'll be sure to take that as some kind of compliment. We're still looking at a plan B option here, right? I really don't want to step on anyone's toes, either the locals or Interpol."

"I totally agree. I think we should forget about having time off and try to find a wig shop. Do you think they'd have such a thing out here?"

"There's only one way to find out." Miranda snatched up her towel and slipped on her shoes. "Don't sit there all day. We have work to do, woman." She walked into the reception area and asked if any of the three people behind the counter spoke English.

"Of course," the youngest woman said, smiling broadly and walking toward the desk. "What can I help you with?"

"I've been invited to a fancy dress party tonight and wondered if there was a shop nearby who rented out outfits for such occasions?"

"Oh, yes. I know of two such places on the main street in the town centre. Do you have a map of the area?"

"No. Is there any chance you could arrange a taxi to pick us up and take us there?"

"Yes, I can do that for you. When would you like to leave?"

"In ten minutes. That's very kind of you."

"Leave it with me. We're here to help if there is ever anything else you need."

Miranda spun on her heel and grabbed Caroline's arm as the chief stepped into reception. "Thank you. We'll bear that in mind," she called over her shoulder to the receptionist.

"What the heck is going on?"

"We've got ten minutes to get to our room, change, and be back down here. No time for chatting. Move!"

Caroline stomped up the two flights of stairs after Miranda, grumbling under her breath most of the way, much to Miranda's amusement.

The taxi dropped them off in the centre of town and promised to wait for them to return. "I hope you're going to be shelling out for the ride on expenses?" Miranda asked.

"You bet. What colour do you fancy becoming?"

They walked into the costume shop and scanned the interior. "I was thinking something like a brunette for a change. Even blondes get fed up with their colour now and again."

"Yeah, but you have so much more fun than us brunettes do. Try this one." Caroline took a long brunette wig off one of the stands and fitted it on Miranda's head.

"Gosh, that does look funny." To Miranda, the change of colour made her appear more intellectual, younger even, which really surprised her.

"Funny in a peculiar kind of way or what?" Caroline asked, studying Miranda's reflection in the mirror.

A shop assistant joined them before she had a chance to answer. The woman started speaking in Portuguese but stopped once she realised Miranda and Caroline weren't following. "Are you English?"

Miranda expelled a large breath. "Yes. We're looking for a wig for a fancy dress party. I like this one, but I'm finding it a little heavy. What do you suggest?"

"It depends what you are going dressed as."

"Oh yes, how silly of me. I haven't really thought that far," Miranda stated before Caroline nudged her in the back. "Can you show us a few outfits to help me decide?"

The woman ran around the shop as if she'd been swept up in a tornado, collecting various outfits off the rails. Every now and again, she would glance at Miranda and back at an outfit before either adding it to the ones draped across her forearm or popping it back on the rail. Eventually, she asked Miranda to join her in the changing room, where she hung the six costumes she'd picked out on the peg, and instructed her to try them on before she drew the curtain across the changing cubicle.

Miranda was tempted to try on the sixties-style dress first, but once she'd slipped it over her head, she knew immediately that it wasn't right for her and swiftly removed it. The second choice was similar to a Greek serving wench's outfit which showed off far too much of her cleavage. Finally, she opted to try on a fifties-style dress that she figured wouldn't look out of place since she'd recently read in a magazine that the style was trending and back in fashion lately. She didn't want to look too out of place if she was going to meet Brad Lawrence, so this one appealed to her in that respect. She swept back the curtain to show Caroline.

"Wow, that is stunning! That pink really suits you."

"I agree," the assistant said. "Now, we just need to find you a suitable wig. You want a brown one, yes?"

"I think so. What about that one over there?" She pointed to a dark-brown wig styled in a chignon.

The assistant crossed the room to collect it. She removed it from the stand and brushed the fringe with her fingers. "Perfect style and colour, I believe." She fastened the wig into position and tucked Miranda's hair underneath it.

The transformation was absolutely remarkable even without makeup.

"Wow, you look a million dollars," Caroline said. "You should take it home with you. Alan would be totally blown away."

Miranda swirled from side to side, watching her reflection. "I'm gobsmacked that an outfit and a wig can make this much difference. Sold, or should I say 'hired,'" she said, smiling broadly at the tiny assistant, who was clasping her tanned hands together in glee.

"Beautiful lady. The outfit and hair only enhances your beauty more. I'll sort out the paperwork."

Caroline stood behind Miranda and gripped her shoulders. "Let's hope we don't get the chance to call on this outfit to do our job for us. There's no way on earth any man would turn down an advance coming from you. Good Lord, can you believe what you're seeing? I know I can't."

CHAPTER NINE

With the outfit paid for and bagged up, the two detectives hopped back in the taxi and returned to the hotel, still giggling at the thought of Alan's reaction if ever he saw Miranda dressed up in the outfit. The girl on reception waved at them and motioned that she wanted a word before they went up to their room.

"Anything wrong?" Miranda asked.

"I have a message for you from a Mr. Tiago Lisboa."

She gave Miranda a slip of paper. "Oops, looks like he wants us back at the station ASAP."

"Crap! When did he ring?" Caroline asked the receptionist.

The woman looked at her watch. "Maybe thirty minutes ago."

Caroline gulped. "Thanks. We better get over there before he sends out a search party for us."

Miranda and Caroline rushed up the stairs to their room and quickly changed into more suitable clothing.

"Do you think we should wear black? Just in case we need to go out on surveillance?" Miranda asked.

"I'm going to. It's a shame you can't put your wig and outfit to good use tonight. What a hoot that would be."

They jumped in another taxi back to the station. A uniformed officer showed them through to the hub, where they found an impatient Tiago waiting, his arms folded and foot tapping.

"Ladies. When I said go back to your hotel rooms for a rest, I didn't expect you to go off sightseeing."

"Sorry. We're here now. What's going on?"

"I made some discreet enquiries at the bar Mr. Lawrence usually frequents, and apparently, he is having some kind of party this evening."

Miranda and Caroline stared at each other, agog. Eventually, Miranda said, "What? A party? For what? Do you know?"

"Mr. Lawrence apparently doesn't need a reason to hold one. It is bizarre timing, no?"

"Very bizarre for a supposed grieving widower," Caroline noted, looking thoughtful.

"I know that look. What are you thinking, Caroline?"

Tiago frowned, looking a little agitated that he was being left out of their thoughts.

"I'm thinking that we should jump on the chance to get in there."

"What's this?" Tiago asked, folding his arms tighter across his rounded stomach.

"This afternoon, we were out getting a disguise for Inspector Carr to wear, not sightseeing."

"I see. May I ask for what reason?"

Caroline shrugged. "As a way of getting in there to see where the land lies. Sorry, English term," she apologised after seeing the puzzled expression sweep across his face. "The inspector and I thought it would be a good idea to get inside the property."

"Again, I ask for what purpose?" A tick had developed in his right eye.

Is he annoyed? He certainly looks annoyed. Not wise to step on the leading investigator's toes. Miranda cleared her throat. "In case the extradition doesn't come to fruition."

"So you want to trap the man. Is that it?" He threw his hands up in the air and said something in his native tongue through clenched teeth.

"Not *trap* exactly. Maybe try to get him to confide in me."

"Which one of you ladies does he know?"

Miranda sighed. "Me."

Again, he huffed and spoke in his own language before he added, "Then it would be ridiculous for you to entertain going into the man's home, disguised or not disguised."

Caroline chortled. "You haven't seen the disguise. Christ, even her own mother wouldn't recognise her, I can assure you."

"I don't care. It is *not* going to happen. Do I make myself clear? The man is a suspected murderer."

"Yes, but we also think he had an accomplice. We have no idea who that accomplice is. It would be great if we could at least find that out," Miranda insisted. She understood Tiago's point of view but also had an agenda of her own.

"So, are you telling me that your interrogation skills aren't very good? If I were to question the man, I know that he would buckle immediately and confess if he had an accomplice or not," Tiago stated cockily.

Miranda felt Lisboa was laughing at her behind his stern exterior. "Interrogation? We prefer to use the term *interview* back in the UK,

Sergeant. We don't consider Gestapo techniques, or anything similar, to be very effective in our neck of the woods."

He grunted like a wild boar. "Maybe you should consider it. You should also have a word with your judges and ask them not to be so lenient with your murderers. How can you let these people out of prison after only serving half the terms they were given?"

Miranda held a hand up to try to stop him. "Hey, you're not asking anything that a copper in the UK hasn't asked him- or herself over a thousand times before when they've seen the likes of Lawrence get off scot-free, believe me."

Caroline nodded, and Tiago seemed to rethink his statement, if only momentarily. Turning on his heel, he grunted again and mumbled something under his breath. When he left the room, Miranda and Caroline relaxed against the wall.

"That went well," Miranda observed, glancing around the room, noting how many of the men put their heads down and got back to work the second Tiago passed them.

"Maybe we should have kept quiet about our plan B, after all. It only seemed to rub him up the wrong way."

Tiago returned to the room with three cups on a tray and placed it on the desk. He gave a brief nod. "I apologise for my outburst. It was unforgiveable of me. It would be better and we would accomplish so much more if we did not fight amongst ourselves."

"I agree. Apology accepted. We intended to introduce our plan only in the event of a problem occurring with the extradition." Miranda smiled, trying her hardest to make it appear natural, not forced.

"I get that. Although, I don't really. Was it your intention to entice him back to the UK?"

"Yes. That was it exactly. Maybe we didn't make ourselves clear enough. I apologise."

Caroline nodded. "I do, too. Now, can we get past this and ask what your intentions are during this party, sergeant?"

"My men are in the process of setting up surveillance equipment. Mr. Lawrence always uses the same catering firm. We have replaced a few members of the catering staff with my team. They will be our eyes and ears at the party. You see, there was no need for you to come up with your plan and spend unnecessary money on a disguise." He issued them with a smug grin.

"We'll see," Miranda said. "Do we know who is attending the party? How many?"

"Anyone and everyone who is famous in the region, as usual when the Lawrences throw a bash. Is that the correct term?"

"Yes, that's correct. Are there a lot of wealthy people in the region?" Miranda enquired.

"Of course. Property prices in the area reflect that wealth, too. You can no longer buy a home in this vicinity for under five hundred thousand euros, at a rough guess."

"Wow, that's some wonga." Caroline whistled.

"Wonga? I don't understand?"

"Sorry. Dosh, money, a healthy budget. I take it a lot of these homes are owned by celebrities, that sort of circuit?"

"Yes. You could, or should, put the Lawrences in that bracket, too. They might not be TV or film celebrities, but they are known worldwide and get involved with the same crowd of people, I suspect."

"Interesting. I never really thought about it like that. I just presumed they would stick to either the fashion industry or the cosmetic side of things. It must have really hurt Brad when his business collapsed despite having those kinds of contacts," Miranda said, her mind churning like an express train.

"You're hinting at the motive for him killing his wife? You think he was jealous of her?" Caroline asked.

"We've got to look somewhere. Why not there? Jealousy or envy, it amounts to the same thing. What if she refused to bail him out when his business started to decline? That would grate on his ego, wouldn't it?"

"Ladies, we can debate this all we like later. This party is about to get under way within the hour, and I'd like to get the team organised well before then, if you don't mind."

Caroline waved a dismissive hand. "Sure, you get on with that and let us know what you want us to do. We'll bounce around some ideas of our own."

Tiago rolled his eyes. "I'll look forward to hearing about your ideas later," he mumbled before departing.

Putting their heads together, Miranda and Caroline jotted down notes of things they should watch out for during the evening ahead. Primarily, they were curious to see if anyone latched onto Brad's side for the evening or if he spent more of his time with certain people.

The team headed off inside a van equipped with high-tech surveillance equipment, the likes of which neither of the British detectives had seen before.

The beauty of having Interpol on hand, I suppose.

The evening had already begun to get dark, which they presumed would go on to help instead of hinder their mission. Miranda and Caroline sat on the small seats, crushed by the other four members of the team, all male.

Either Tiago or one of his men did them the courtesy of naming the couples as they arrived at the villa for the soirée. Miranda noted down the names, none of which she recognised. *So much for the famous celebrities attending in droves.*

The time dragged by, and all the attendees at the bash seemed to be on their best behaviour until at least an hour into the party. The volume of the music suddenly rose, filling the night air with the thumping sound of rhythmic base. Miranda, ever one to enjoy people-watching, picked up a pair of binoculars and studied Lawrence, who was busy circulating the room and chatting with his guests. Around this time, a lone woman joined the party. She was taller than most of the other women in the room and thin enough to border on the skinny side, but she was beautifully dressed and manicured. As she glided into the room, many of the men watched her, their mouths dropped open in awe, prompting their partners to either slap their arms or dig them in the ribs.

"Any idea who she is?" Miranda offered the binoculars to Tiago.

He took them from her and zoomed in for a closer look. "I'm unsure at this time. Anyone else recognise the woman?"

The rest of the team shook their heads.

"Did she come alone? Did anyone even see her arrive? I didn't, and I've been watching the arrivals like a hawk," Caroline asked.

Tiago translated the chief's question to the other team members, and the answer surprised everyone. No one had seen the mysterious woman arrive.

"How strange. Do you think she was already at the property? Maybe she's a friend helping out with organising the event? Tiago, can you possibly ask someone on the inside who she is?" Miranda eyed the woman again through the glasses.

"Not at the moment. All the undercover men are busy. We'll have to wait until they contact us during their break."

The team waited on tenterhooks until that time presented itself. Miranda's gaze remained fixed on the woman until the word came in. The woman always seemed to be within easy reach of Brad, and Miranda noticed the way his elbow brushed her breasts when he moved around the room. Their glances held each other's as if they were holding a secret conversation, sparking Miranda to feel uneasy. "I'm not liking this, Caroline. There's something going on between those two."

"We need to find out who she is first. Any idea when your guys will get a break, Tiago? The frustration of not knowing who she is will be the death of me." Caroline leaned over and extracted the binoculars from Miranda's hands.

Tiago laughed. "You two ladies need to show some restraint. Do you not know the meaning of the word *patience*?"

"We've been bloody patient for the last couple of hours. It's wearing a tad thin now," the chief snapped back. Her words were accompanied by one of her renowned smiles, which did little to disguise how irritated she was becoming.

Ignoring her tone, Tiago turned back to the monitors to watch the interactions going on at the party. Eventually, he clasped a headset over his thinning hair and spoke in Portuguese, stopping only briefly to listen to his contact's answers.

"Shesh… let the guy get a word in, buster," Caroline complained out of the corner of her mouth.

Miranda stifled a grin when Tiago looked sharply at the chief.

"Oops, guess that slipped out louder than I intended."

Miranda covered her mouth with her hand.

Tiago disconnected his call and swivelled in his chair to look at them. "I have a name for you. Vanessa Estevez, and from what my team are telling me, she was already at the villa when they started their shift. She changed for the party upstairs while the other partygoers arrived."

Miranda nodded. "Do they know where she got changed?"

"Does it really matter?" Tiago frowned.

"Yes. If she got changed in the master bedroom, then we can safely assume they are an item. On the other hand, if she bathed and dressed in the guest bedroom, then perhaps her involvement is more along the lines of a friend helping out. Although, saying that, what

I've observed of the couple so far this evening, I'm still inclined to believe they are lovers."

"I see you think situations through thoroughly, Inspector. Good for you. I suggest we carry on observing the couple for this evening and then assess everything fully in the morning, agreed?"

Miranda and Caroline both nodded reluctantly and relaxed back in their chairs, continuing to observe the partygoers with added interest as the alcohol they were drinking began to take effect. Before long, the guests made their way out to the brightly lit pool area. Frivolous party games ensued, most of which ended up with the participants taking a dip in the pool.

Miranda cringed. "God, I hope we don't end up witnessing some kind of swingers' event."

Caroline laughed and tilted her head back when Tiago asked what she meant.

Blushing, Miranda enlightened the sergeant. "Swingers, wife swappers, people getting off with other people's partners. Don't make me go into detail any more than that, please."

Tiago's mouth twisted into a smile. "Thank you. I'll make sure I add that word to my vocabulary."

"I wouldn't bother if I were you. Do you get much of that kind of action going on out here?"

"Not that I'm aware of, but then, who knows what goes on behind closed doors?"

"That's true enough. I hope things don't drift into that kind of thing." Miranda leaned over and whispered to Caroline, "I don't fancy witnessing any real-life porn, do you? Do you think we should get out of here before things deteriorate?"

"Nope. I think we should be here until the party ends."

"You're kidding?" Miranda folded her arms crossly when she heard Tiago and his men sniggering. *Great, well, this isn't my idea of a fun evening.*

The partygoers thankfully restrained themselves from going too far and began to dwindle away from the premises around three thirty in the morning. Once everyone had gone home and only Brad, the woman, and the staff remained to clear up the mess, Tiago insisted the mission was over.

"Can we get a taxi near here, Sergeant?" Caroline asked.

"There's no need. We will drop you back at the hotel before we take the van off at the station."

The van pulled away from the scene and arrived at the hotel a few minutes later. "May I propose we join up at the station's incident room at nine a.m. promptly, ladies?"

"We'll be there, bright eyed and raring to go" Caroline assured him.

Once they were in their hotel room, dressed in their pyjamas and ready for bed, they quickly ran through the night's activities then decided to switch out the light. Miranda drifted off to sleep around four, and her dreams were full of images from the soirée, more importantly of pictures of Lawrence and this strange beauty. Hopefully, they would get a clearer indication about her in the morning.

CHAPTER TEN

Miranda sat forward, concentrating on the flipchart Tiago was standing beside. He conducted the meeting mainly in Portuguese, picking out the main points in English for the benefit of his British guests.

"What do we know about this Estevez woman, Sergeant?" Caroline asked when Tiago looked to be winding up the meeting.

The sergeant tutted noisily. "I was just coming to that, Chief Inspector."

"And?" Caroline urged impatiently, adding to the man's annoyance.

"I'm still trying to gather all the information. I intend returning to the bar this morning when they open and asking if the barman knows of this woman and their relationship. So far, the man hasn't let me down. Would you like to come with me?"

"Excellent, what a great idea." Caroline smiled at the sergeant. "I'd still like us to question the neighbours in light of what we saw last night, too. Would that be acceptable to you?"

"Whatever you like, Chief Inspector. I have an idea that you will do it anyway, with or without my authorisation."

"Bravo, that's very astute of you. Umm… I don't suppose you have a note about chasing up the extradition order on your to-do list for today, have you?"

"It's at the top of the list of my priorities," Tiago said.

"Great. Any chance we can contact London in a moment?" Miranda asked, gazing sideways at Caroline.

"Of course. Right, do you mind if I finalise this meeting now?"

"Go right ahead." Caroline leaned over and whispered, "Why are you contacting the station?"

"Well, I thought I'd get the ball rolling and send Johnny a picture of the woman. He can start the investigation going at that end."

"Good thinking. I'll get us some coffee."

Miranda picked up the phone and dialled the station.

Johnny sounded out of breath when he answered her call. "Ma'am, sorry, I've just got in. You're ringing early."

"Am I? Shit, sorry, I forgot about the hour's difference. How are things going back there? Is everyone pitching in?"

"Yep. They're all being surprisingly amicable towards me. Not sure how long that's likely to last, though. What can I do for you? Oh wait, just a sec…"

Miranda heard her partner open an envelope and groan. "Johnny? What's going on?"

"DNA results from the car. I was groaning because of the work I predict ahead of us."

"Meaning? What does it say?"

"It appears that Brad's car was indeed used to transport the body. It also says that a knife was found in the boot of the car and that initial tests show three sets of prints on the handle."

"Really? Any idea who they belong to? I'm guessing Anneka and Brad's would likely be on there, but not sure who the third set would belong to."

"Yep, two sets belong to the husband and wife. The third set, they're running through the system now. Probably the maid or whatever she's classed as, you think?" Johnny replied.

"Maybe. Listen, I'm going to fax you a photo of a person of interest, a female who I think is more than just an acquaintance to Brad."

"Okay. What do you propose I do with it?"

Miranda let out a long breath. "First, I need you to go back to Anneka's flats in the city and show the neighbours the photo."

"Right, to see if she's visited the flat? Realistically, would she have done that while Anneka was still alive? Or are you suggesting she was possibly a friend to both of them?"

"I don't really know what I'm suggesting at the moment, Johnny. Just humour me for now. Keep chasing forensics about that unknown print, too. Tell them to widen the search and go international if need be. Looking at the number of friends who turned up at their party last night, it could be that one of these nice people aided Brad in either the murdering of his wife or at least the disposal of her body."

"Ah, I get you. Okay, any idea when you'll be back?"

"We're not sat around by the pool all day, if that's what you're implying, matey."

"I wasn't. Why do you always have to twist my words, boss?"

"And when did you lose your sense of humour? I was joking. We're chasing up the extradition order now, but if that fails, the chief and I have come up with a little plan that could hook the bugger anyway. We'll let you know what happens on that front. Ring me if you get any other news, okay?"

"Yep. I'll wait for the fax to come through and visit the flats this morning. I don't suppose you have a name for the woman?"

"Sorry, yes. Vanessa Estevez, and we're presuming she's Portuguese."

"That'll help. I'll speak to you later."

"We'll be here at the station all day."

Caroline shook her head vehemently to correct her.

"Oops, no, we won't. We'll be in and out, trying to gather information on this woman in the local vicinity. Call me around five your time, okay?"

"Sure, that suits me fine."

"Good luck."

"Yeah, you, too."

Miranda hung up. "They found a knife in the car. They think it's *the* knife that killed Anneka." She scanned the room looking for a picture she could possibly send back to the UK.

"So I gathered. Three sets of prints. Is that right?"

"Let me sort this fax out, and then we'll discuss it. Tiago, do you have a clear picture of this Estevez woman, please?"

He searched a file on the desk closest to him and approached her with a ten-by-eight glossy photo. Miranda studied the picture for a moment or two, trying to determine what was going on behind the woman's startling ocean-blue eyes. "What are you hiding, lady?"

"That's what we'll hopefully find out very soon." Tiago smiled reassuringly at Miranda.

"All right if I use the fax? I want my partner in London to revisit a couple of Anneka's neighbours. He can ask them if they recognise the woman. If they do, then we can put her down as a possible accomplice to the crime."

"Good thinking, Inspector. Come with me. I'll show you where the fax is."

"Will we be setting off for the bar soon?" Miranda asked as they left the room.

"There is no need to go too early. I intend leaving around eleven. Until then, I want to keep going through the information we collected last night and do some serious searching into the guests' backgrounds."

"Don't forget to chase up the order, too."

He stopped, and she stuttered to a halt alongside him. "Inspector, will you do me the courtesy of not repeating yourself. I'm well aware of the urgency behind the order, but experience has told me that if you pester the judges, they always put your file to the bottom of the pile. Just be patient for a few days—he's not going anywhere, and my men have him under constant surveillance."

"Just put me down as a control freak, Tiago. I apologise."

He started walking again and chuckled. "I feel sorry for Mr. Carr, in that case."

Miranda laughed, despite trying not to. "There isn't a Mr. Carr yet. Although, we're working on it. I should be at home now, sorting out the wedding, which is due to take place next month. However, my DCI had other plans. I think she thought this would be a breeze and we'd be stretched out by the pool all day while Brad was tucked up in a cell."

"Clearly, she thought wrong. Although, you did manage to spend some time by the pool yesterday, did you not?"

"I guess. Be honest with me—how long do you think it will be before we can arrest Brad?"

"At least another two to three days. So you might go back to the UK with a useful tan for your wedding yet."

They reached the fax machine, sent the photo to Johnny, then headed back to the incident room, where both ladies ended up twiddling their thumbs before Tiago snapped his fingers and ordered them to join him.

Pulling faces behind the rude sergeant's back amused the other members of the team no end. The three of them left the station and jumped in the sergeant's own car.

"It would be better if we turned up in this rather than a police car, I think. You see? I do have some sense, detectives."

"Neither of us doubted that for a second, Sergeant," Miranda assured him.

The small bar, situated a few roads south of the Lawrence villa, was very quiet when they got there. Two elderly gentlemen sat in the window seat, sipping at their small cups of coffee while putting the world to rights. Tiago instructed Miranda and Caroline to take a seat, then he shook hands with the bar owner and conducted a quiet conversation with him. The sergeant joined them, carrying three cups of coffee, about ten minutes later.

"Well?" Caroline asked impatiently the second the sergeant took his seat.

His eyes widened, and he leaned in to whisper, "Well. That was rather informative."

"Jesus, man, get on with it?" Caroline said through clenched teeth.

Miranda nudged her boss. "Give him a chance to take a breath, Caroline."

The chief threw herself back in the chair and folded her arms petulantly. She soon shuffled forward again when Tiago started telling them what he'd learned.

"According to my friend over there, when I showed him the picture of the woman, things began to slot into place."

"In what way?" Miranda's interest piqued considerably.

"He said that he believed this woman had been friends with Brad for a few months now."

"A few months? Did Anneka know this?" Caroline asked.

"Not at first. But she did find out about 'their friendship' a few weeks ago."

"Well, that sounds like a possible motive for murder if ever I heard one." Miranda took a sip from her cup then shook her head at the strength of the coffee. "What else did he say? Is she local? Does he know of her or her background?"

"I didn't want to seem too aggressive in my questioning. He gave me enough to work with for now."

"Do you think she's staying at the villa permanently, Tiago? Did you get that out of him, at least?"

"She's a constant visitor at the house. One of his acquaintances runs a small supermarket, and Brad's visitor rings up frequently, wanting groceries delivered. He's not sure if that means she has moved in permanently or not. He was shocked when I told him Anneka's body had been found." He raised a hand at their horrified gasps. "Do not worry, I trust him. He won't spread that news around, I assure you. If he does, he knows that he might as well say goodbye to his business at the end of the week."

Miranda's eyes bulged. "Wow, you have the power to do that?"

"No. But it doesn't do any harm dropping a subtle hint in that vein."

"So, where do we go from here? Get a warrant for her arrest, too?"

"I think so. I haven't told you the best part yet. The local gossip is that the couple have been in the UK together."

"What? Did they both return at the same time?"

"It appears so, yes." Tiago nodded.

"And there we have it. Yet another motive for murder, if indeed the couple were carrying on." Miranda sat back in her chair and started to turn her cup in the saucer.

"Well, it appears that they've been pretty brazen about their relationship so far. Jesus, I'd say it was a probable motive and some," Caroline quickly agreed.

"Then, if we're all in agreement, we should arrest the woman at the same time."

Miranda ran a hand over her chin and tutted before shooting down his idea. "That's all well and good, Tiago, but you have nothing concrete against the woman other than her being Brad's acquaintance. In our country, that is *not* an arrestable offence."

"Then we have a serious dilemma on our hands, ladies. If we arrest and extradite Lawrence, there is every likelihood that the woman will abscond and not look back."

"Possibly. On the other hand, if they're head over hills in love, she might prefer to stand by her man and follow him to London again, especially if we don't let on that we suspect them of having an affair or of her having any involvement in the wife's murder. We'll just need to be as cunning as they've been, won't we?"

They consumed the rest of coffee in silence as each of them considered the limited options available. They left the bar twenty minutes later, just as the locals and a few of the holidaymakers started filtering in for a late breakfast or early lunch.

"That reminds me—we skipped breakfast this morning." Miranda looked up and down the road and spotted a baker's shop on the opposite side. "Mind if we grab a roll to take back with us?"

"Good idea. We could be in for a long afternoon. I want to ensure all angles are covered. I'm not keen on letting this lady escape our grasp, and we need to come up with a plan to trap her."

"Agreed. Shall I buy rolls for everyone?" Miranda asked, ready to dart across the road between the oncoming cars.

"Yes, I will sort you out with some money when we get back to the station."

Miranda played it safe and bought ten ham rolls, opting to buy more than was needed rather than risking the team complaining they were hungry during the rest of the afternoon.

The team worked hard and were thorough in their investigations into the other partygoers but didn't find anything useful. The phone rang just before they decided to call it a day.

Tiago held it out for Miranda to take. "Your partner."

"Hi, Johnny. Any news for us?"

The room fell silent, and every set of eyes turned to her, making her feel slightly uncomfortable.

"Well, I did as you asked and visited both flats. The apartment manager at the flat in the centre of the city said that he'd never laid eyes on the woman before. But there was better news at the other flat. The manager there remembers seeing the woman once or twice and even recollected her visiting Brad the day before he left for Portugal."

"Visited as in came and left or visited as in stayed overnight at the residence?"

"He wasn't sure. So... I took the liberty of ringing the airline again and asked if they had a seat booking in the name of Estevez on the same flight as Lawrence. They did."

"Any news on that print yet, Johnny?"

"Not yet. I'll chase it up again tomorrow and keep chasing until I get an answer, if you like."

"Yep, just keep making a nuisance of yourself. Mind you, if they're running it through worldwide systems, it is bound to take a while before a result shows up. Good work, matey. Are you off home soon?"

"Another hour or so. We're behind you, remember? Just going through some of your crappy paperwork now. How the bloody hell do you cope with this crap on a daily basis?"

"Ah, the joys of being an inspector. Filling in for a few days is enough to put anyone off applying for the job, right?"

"Affirmative on that one, boss. I better let you get on with your evening. I'll ring you tomorrow if I hear anything else. Will you do the same if the extradition gets the clearance?"

"Of course. Thanks, Johnny. Goodnight." Miranda replaced the phone in its docking station and relayed the information to the onlookers.

Tiago nodded. "Okay. Well, that's a positive then. Thinking about things seriously for a moment, I propose that when we finally arrest Lawrence, we ignore the woman completely, due to lack of evidence. My impression is that all she seems to be guilty of is being fixated with Lawrence. Is that the right word?" he asked Miranda.

"I'd be more inclined to say she was besotted with him."

"Ah yes. Thank you. Lawrence appears to have the woman where he wants her, and had she not been involved in the crime of murder, I think she would have been scared off by now. The fact that she's very much in his life suggests they are both in the shit up to their necks. However, a word of caution—as we've determined already, *without evidence*, we cannot arrest the woman. Any idea when that set of prints is due back, Inspector?"

She shrugged. "No idea. Maybe it was smudged or only a partial print. That would explain the delay. My partner never mentioned if the print was intact or not, and I forgot to ask, sorry. Can I make a suggestion regarding the woman?"

"Of course. Go on." Tiago tilted his head and sat on the edge of the nearby desk.

"What if we arrest Lawrence. Play all nice with her, not indicate that we know she might be involved. Leave the villa but have one of your men remain close by, ready to tail her. I just wish we still had eyes and ears on what's going on inside the villa."

"Unfortunately, all our surveillance gear was attached either to the undercover cops or the equipment used at the function."

"That's a shame. It would have been better if one of your men had at least bugged the place. Would you be agreeable to a man tailing her, though? Do you have the resources for that?"

Tiago rested his head on a fist and stretched out his forefinger as he thought over the plan. "It makes perfect sense, and I'll action it immediately once we arrest Lawrence. The best thing to do is for us to act casually towards this woman, not to raise her suspicions that we are lining her up as being his accomplice. Yes, I think that could work, and I'm sorry about the bug. I feel bad about that. We had little time to arrange things as it was, and it slipped my mind."

Miranda and Caroline bid the rest of the team goodbye and took a taxi back to the hotel.

"Fancy a dip in the pool?" the chief asked in the reception area.

She glanced out through the large windows. Tempted by the cool blue water, she shook her head. "No costume, remember? You go dangle your feet. I'll ring Alan if that's okay and catch up with you afterwards."

Caroline swiftly changed into her shorts and T-shirt and left the room.

Miranda removed her shoes, stretched out on the bed, and dialled home. Alan picked up after the first ring.

"Hello, sweetheart. That was quick."

"I was just passing the phone on my way into the kitchen to fix dinner. I miss you."

"I miss you, too. Hopefully, we'll be back home within a few days." She smiled, closed her eyes, and imagined him lying next to her.

"That's a relief. I never thought it would be possible to miss someone so much. I know Mum and Dad were inseparable, but I never thought I'd end up the same. I suppose that's a good thing, right? That's what I keep trying to tell myself anyway when I'm cuddling your pillow at night."

"It's certainly wonderful to hear. Does a girl's ego the world of good. Maybe we can spend some quality time together when I get back, go away to that lovely country hotel? We haven't splashed out on anything like that in a while because of the wedding."

"Sounds like a great idea to me. Won't you have a lot of paperwork and that to catch up on when you get back into town?"

"Yes, but that can wait. Spending time with you is my main priority, or it will be once I'm back. Have you heard from Mum?"

"Yes, she rang to let us know that she's got everything planned out, and she's managed to get superb deals from the suppliers, too."

"Fantastic. I think we'll need to cut costs where we can in the coming weeks. What are you having for dinner?"

"I treated myself to a bit of steak. I hope that was okay. A tad extravagant of me, I know."

"Don't be silly. Hey, I'll have the same here, hopefully that'll help ease your guilt. How's that?"

"Deal."

"Okay, I was just touching base with you. I better go and see what problems Caroline is causing down by the pool."

"Throw that in just to make me jealous, eh? It worked. Ring me when you know what day you're coming home."

"I will. Love you." She blew him a kiss, and he returned the gesture before they hung up.

Invigorated, she scrambled off the bed and slipped into her shorts and T-shirt. She picked up the room key and ran down the stairs to join Caroline, who was sitting on the edge of the pool, dangling her legs in the water. Again, the area was surprisingly empty, given the time of day.

Miranda approached the edge and tentatively placed one foot in the pool. She quickly adjusted to the cool water.

"Everything all right back at home?" Caroline asked, making small whirlpools with her feet.

"Yep. Lover Boy is missing his lady, though."

"Aw... ain't love grand?" As quick as a flash, Caroline pushed Miranda towards the water.

"Don't you bloody dare!"

"Too late. The force is with me." Caroline pushed harder, and Miranda toppled headfirst into the water.

Spluttering, trying to catch her breath without taking in more chlorine, Miranda thrashed violently, sending large waves of water over Caroline's bare legs. Then she grabbed Caroline's ankles and yanked her into the pool. The two women screeched and carried on with their petty game for another five minutes until, worn out, both of them swam to the side, gasping for breath.

"What shall we do for dinner tonight?" Caroline asked, her back against the edge of the pool, letting her legs float in front of her.

"What about asking the receptionist if we can get room service? Not sure I fancy getting dried off and dressed up again after the day we've had. Anyway, I'm running out of clothes fast, thanks to your practical jokes."

"Sour-faced mare. Room service sounds good to me. We could see if there's a film on this evening and veg out in front of the box."

"In Portuguese? We wouldn't understand the plot."

"Ah, that's my plan. You see, we could make up a plot of our own as we go along."

"You're nuts." Miranda stepped out of the pool, squeezed as much water as she could out of her clothes, and wrapped her towel around herself.

The receptionist was happy to oblige their room service request and directed them to the menu in their room.

"Can we just order chicken piri piri and chips for two now. Is that all right?" Caroline asked cheekily.

"I wanted steak." Miranda stared at her friend, confounded that she had ordered for her.

"Everyone eats steak in hotels when they're on holiday. Be more adventurous. Eat like a local for a change."

"Smartarse."

After showering and settling down on the bed, they tucked into the surprisingly good meal. Miranda turned on the TV and flicked through the Portuguese channels, searching for any English news. She paused when she spotted Anneka's smiling face on the screen. Turning up the volume, Miranda dropped her fork.

The newscaster was saying what a great shame it was that the woman who had created such a remarkable cosmetic empire, lost her life only days before the launch of the company's newest product. The screen filled with snapshots from the launch party, and Miranda pointed out Jess and Sheila to Caroline, who seemed happy enough about how the launch had turned out.

"I'm glad Sheila looks happy. It must be a very bittersweet moment for her. She has the funeral to deal with in the next few days, too. I hope we're back in time for that. I'd really like to show my support by attending the service." Her appetite having wavered, Miranda placed her plate to the side.

"I'm sure we'll be back in London by then. Not sure I would have been able to cope with the media as well as Sheila has. She has to be admired for pulling off that wee miracle."

The news story ended with a shot of Jess and Sheila hugging, tears streaming down their faces as they glanced up at a huge banner emblazoned with a picture of Anneka watching over them, holding a raised glass of champagne. Miranda's eyes misted up, and she searched her handbag for a tissue. "It's just so sad. The woman had everything to live for. To have her life extinguished by a person she loved, and who supposedly loved her, is just too abhorrent for words."

"I agree. There's no point dwelling on how sad the case is, though, Miranda; every case we deal with is a sad event. I think you're more perturbed about letting Lawrence abscond. Well, you need to stop thinking that way and start putting all your—*our* energy and resourcefulness into bringing the culprit to justice. I, for one, am going to enjoy seeing the look on Brad's face when that order is served on him. No one is going to prevent us from being there to see that happen."

Puzzled, Miranda looked at her friend. "Do you think Tiago will do that? Arrest him in our absence?"

"I have no idea, but I intend to stick to that man like glue from now on, at work anyway. Just in case the thought does cross his mind."

CHAPTER ELEVEN

The next three days turned out to be the most irritating days Miranda had ever experienced during her career. Caroline certainly seemed to feel the same. Finally, just after two o'clock in the afternoon on the third day, Tiago received the call that the extradition order had been granted.

Practically overtaken by a force of nature, he ran around the office, issuing orders to the team. Eventually, Miranda placed a hand on his arm and handed him a cup of coffee. "You need to slow down, Tiago. Take a breath, man."

"It's what we've been waiting for. Aren't you excited?"

"Of course, but there's no point in all of us running around like headless chickens. You're displaying enough excitement on our behalf. What happens after his arrest? Should the chief and I go and pack our bags, be ready for a flight out of here?"

"Yes—no, I mean wait until after we have him in custody. You do want to be there when he's arrested, don't you?"

"Too right, we do," Caroline intervened. "How long before we go to the villa?"

"The courier should be here within the hour. We'll go immediately once we have the document in our hands."

"Okay. We'll sit and wait until then." Miranda slouched back in her chair as Tiago walked away.

Caroline patted Miranda's knee. "Stop worrying. It won't take us long to pack our bags."

"I know. Mind if I nip out for a walk? I could do with some fresh air. I'll only be about ten minutes."

"Sure, as long as that's all it is."

Miranda stretched her legs. She wasn't really one for hanging around, waiting for opportunities to come her way.

Upon her return, she recognised the buzz in the room had heightened to another level. Each member of the team was pacing his or her individual space. Finally, Tiago proudly announced he had the paper they were anxiously waiting for. The whole team left the station and jumped into three cars. The convoy set off for the villa with Tiago, Caroline, and Miranda in the lead vehicle. As they approached the villa, Miranda's stomach twisted and turned into large knots, and her heart rate quickened. She hoped Anneka was with them in spirit, smiling at what was about to take place.

The officer on surveillance duty left his post and joined the rest of the team when the cars pulled up outside the main gate. Tiago asked the man if Lawrence had left the house that morning—he hadn't. The sergeant pressed the buzzer on the intercom. "Mr. Lawrence, it's Sergeant Tiago Lisboa from Interpol. Please open the gates. I'd like a word with you."

Miranda nudged Caroline when the four-letter expletive that left Lawrence's mouth travelled over the intercom.

Still, the gates remained closed.

"Mr. Lawrence, this is your final warning. Open the gates now, or we will break them down and enter the property by force. The choice is yours."

After a few seconds of silence, the metal railing gates slowly swung open. Tiago drove through them before the man had a chance to change his mind. "Ladies, please do not interfere with the proceedings. You are here merely as observers. Is that understood?"

"We understand. Can you make sure that you'll be careful what you say in front of Estevez? As you've already suggested, it's important not to alert her in the slightest," Miranda said.

He nodded. "She's going to be alarmed by the events. Hopefully, she will have the sense to keep out of trouble. If not, then we will have to arrest her. We'll see. Here we go."

Lawrence was waiting for them on the front step of his house. As the team climbed out of the vehicles, his eyes connected with Miranda. He visibly deflated and retreated into the house. Several of the larger members of the team ran after him. He struggled and shouted, twisted and kicked out, but the two men on either side of him held his arms firmly.

"Mr. Lawrence, I am here to arrest you for the murder of Anneka Lawrence." Tiago continued to read the man his rights as Brad's face drained of all colour.

"You're wrong. I loved my wife. I didn't kill her." He proceeded to spout his innocence, to no avail. "Inspector, you know how distraught I was when Anneka died. Please tell them they are making a mistake."

"Plead all you like, Brad. In my book, a grieving widower wouldn't be holding parties for his friends a few days after his dearly departed wife's death. Oh, and by the way, I explicitly instructed you *not* to leave the country. That dumb manoeuvre only highlighted your involvement in your wife's murder. Maybe if you'd stayed put in London, the case would have still remained unsolved. Foolish act, Brad. Murderers need to be craftier than that if they want to get away with their crimes."

"I'm innocent, I tell you. What proof do you have that an intruder didn't kidnap my wife and kill her?"

Miranda rubbed her chin between her thumb and forefinger. "Proof—well, that'll be the fact we have your car in a forensic lab at present, going through all sorts of tests." She paused to prolong the man's agony and stifled a smile when his eyes almost dropped out of his head. "Ah, then of course there's the murder weapon, the knife found in the boot of your car. Yes, it all adds up nicely, Brad. Tardiness on your part, but superb detecting skills on mine."

"You've planted it. All the clues, they're down to you being mischievous. In line for a promotion, are you? The brown-nosing not enough for your superiors? Is that what this is all about?"

Caroline took a menacing step forward, until her nose almost touched his. "I'd keep your mouth shut if I were you, Mr. Lawrence. Of course, you could always ignore my advice and add to the charges already lying at your door."

"You can't pin anything on me. *Nothing*. Anyway, your jurisdiction doesn't cover Portugal, you dumb bitches."

Caroline roared with laughter and gestured to Tiago. "That's where the sergeant comes in. Did you miss the part where he said he was from Interpol, Lawrence? You'll be winging your way back to the UK before the day is out, thanks to the extradition order we have managed to secure with your name printed on it."

Miranda was surprised Tiago had let them have their say despite his prior warning that they were to remain mere observers, maybe he had reconsidered his warning given that the suspect was a fellow countryman of hers—he simply waved the paper in Lawrence's face to emphasise the chief's point.

Brad slouched against the men restraining him, seemingly giving up the fight. Miranda was suspicious and silently urged the men not to loosen their grip on him once he was outside. She found it hard to believe that they hadn't even slapped the handcuffs on him yet. *I hope they don't regret their tardiness.*

As she surveyed the hallway, her gaze drifted up to the landing just in time to see a wisp of fabric disappear. She nudged Caroline, nodded towards the spot, and whispered, "We're being spied on."

"Run, Vanessa, run," Brad shouted.

"Dumb move, dickhead," Caroline said, prodding Brad Lawrence's forehead.

In the confusion, Brad escaped the men's grasps, immediately reached for a nearby bottle of wine, smashed it on the edge of the table and grabbed Caroline around the throat. He placed the jagged glass against her neck, nicking her skin. Jumping ahead of Tiago, and his men standing nearby, Miranda took charge of the situation. "Don't be foolish, Brad. Let the chief go, and we promise you lenience at your trial. Hurt her, and you'll be damaging your own future."

"What future? What kind of idiot do you bloody take me for? The only upside of you arresting me is that there is no longer a death penalty in the UK. Back off, or I'll stab her in the jugular and let her bleed out."

Miranda held her arms out to the side, preventing the team from attempting to race forward to overpower Lawrence. She'd dealt with crazies in this kind of situation all her working life. "Brad, listen to me before it's too late. Surrender now. The longer this goes on, the worse it's going to look in a judge's eyes. Come on, man."

Brad's forearm tightened around the chief's neck. Caroline grabbed his arm, trying to release the grip while she gasped for breath.

"Okay, okay. Loosen your grip on her. She can't breathe. Do you want another death on your conscience?"

"Back off, the fuckin' lot of you. Put the keys to your car in my pocket," he instructed one of the nearby officers whilst pulling his forearm tighter around Caroline's throat emphasising his point for the officer not to try anything dumb. Miranda noticed her friend's colour turning almost blue.

Miranda's pulse raced. *Think girl, think. You've got to get Caroline out of this mess.* "Brad, what about if we sort out a plea bargain for you? Was Anneka's death an accident perhaps? We can go along those lines. Just let the chief go, please?"

When Brad didn't look as if he was going to change his mind, Tiago reluctantly ordered his officer to hand over the keys.

The gesture made Miranda cry out. "No! Don't go, Brad. Don't do this."

But it was too late. He dragged Caroline's almost-limp body through the front door. Miranda heard a noise from upstairs. She bolted up the staircase and into the main bedroom, only to see Vanessa shimmying down the vine covering the front of the building. Miranda ran back through the bedroom and shouted, "Don't let them get away."

Finally Miranda snapped. Infuriated that the team of men were discussing what to do next rather than leaping into action, she pushed Tiago towards the main entrance. "Do something. Disable the car somehow, for fuck's sake! Caroline, I won't let him take you." She scanned the area quickly then dived into Tiago's pocket and extracted his keys. "Call yourself no-nonsense policemen? You're pathetic, the lot of you."

The insult appeared to do the trick. The team, including Tiago, finally reacted. He snatched the keys back from Miranda and ordered his men with instructions in Portuguese. Luckily, loading up the car had hindered Lawrence's getaway. Miranda watched on as the cars they'd arrived in spun their wheels and rushed to block the getaway car from leaving the driveway. *Shit! Please don't get Caroline hurt in the process. Proceed with caution. I don't want my best friend hurt—I could never forgive myself.*

Lawrence's car screeched to a halt. The passenger door opened, and Caroline's feet connected with the gravel. She was just about to leave the car when Lawrence grabbed her throat again. This time, things were different. Tiago snatched open the driver's door and gave Lawrence a right hook worthy of a heavyweight boxer. In the following kerfuffle, Miranda ran forward, pushed Caroline back against the seat, and sank her teeth into Lawrence's arm. Then Tiago dragged him from the car. Miranda helped Caroline out of the vehicle then opened the back door. Vanessa had kept out of the melee and was sitting in the backseat, looking gobsmacked, which surprised Miranda. She thought the woman would be screaming at them to let Lawrence go. *The plot thickens! Maybe she is an innocent party in this, after all.*

As soon as Lawrence was standing upright, the officers slapped the cuffs on him. *Better late than never, I suppose.*

Caroline rubbed at her neck and fixed Tiago with an angry glare across the roof of the car. "Shame you didn't fucking slap the cuffs on him inside the house. Bloody amateurs!" She stormed off in a huff.

Miranda followed her inside the house and sought out the drinks cabinet in the corner of the lounge. She filled a large tumbler with whiskey and handed the crystal glass to the chief. "Drink this. It'll ease the embarrassment at least."

Caroline tried to glare at her but broke down in a fit of giggles instead. "What is wrong with these bloody men? Neither you nor I would have forgotten to truss Lawrence up as soon as we arrested him."

"The funny thing is, I was thinking the same thing just before he grabbed you. Maybe I'm as much at fault as them for not prompting them to cuff him the second we arrived."

"What's done is done. I wonder if we can throw Lawrence in a cage and let him travel back to England in the luggage compartment with the rest of the other animals onboard the flight."

"We can ask. I'm not relishing the idea of sitting alongside him or cuffed to him for hours after the trick he's just pulled—that's for sure." Miranda glanced out the window to see the rest of the team shoving Lawrence around between them. The whole thing looked farcical, like some kind of kid's party game where the person in the middle ended up giddy. "What in God's name? I think you were right calling them amateurs. That kind of behaviour would never be seen on our patch. Drink up, let's try and intervene and get home as soon as we can. I've had enough of this place to turn me off Portugal for life."

"I'm with you on that one. Next time I volunteer to come with you on a mission, remind me of this incident, will you?" Caroline gulped down the amber liquid, slammed the glass down on the counter, and wiped her mouth with the back of her hand.

Outside, as soon as they laid eyes on the two British detectives, the men called a halt to their juvenile game and placed Lawrence in the back of one of the cars. Caroline and Miranda hopped in the back of Tiago's car without saying a word. The sergeant took the hint at how annoyed the women were and slipped behind the wheel. He drove in silence to the station, where Lawrence was thrown into a police cell. Vanessa Estevez was taken into an interview room, then Tiago questioned her for three hours straight. He joined the rest of the team in the incident room and shared his insight about the woman.

"To me, Vanessa Estevez is innocent in this matter. She went along with Lawrence because she became besotted with the man. She had no idea he ever intended to kill his wife and has agreed to fly to England to testify in the case against him."

Miranda and Caroline exchanged puzzled looks.

"Really?" Miranda whispered to the chief. "It's as simple as that?"

"Maybe he has a way with women that neither of us have witnessed or appreciated. Seems a bit off to me. Don't say anything. We'll pick up the pieces when we're back in the UK."

"What if she doesn't come to England? What if she's trying to pull a fast one?" Miranda asked.

Caroline thought for a moment then raised her hand to interrupt Tiago, who had begun issuing his team with instructions for wrapping up the case. "If I might ask a simple question, Sergeant?"

Tiago made his way towards them. "Yes, Chief Inspector. Fire away."

"What guarantees do we have that Ms. Estevez won't take a flight in the opposite direction once she feels the heat is off her?"

"She has assured me that will not be the case. That is enough for me, Chief Inspector."

Caroline sat back in her chair and folded her arms. The redness around her neck from the earlier entanglement with Lawrence was still very visible. "Really? Again, your gullibility is beyond me, Sergeant, given what has already happened today. Maybe if the attack had been on one of your *men*, we wouldn't be having this conversation right now. Perhaps I should go over your head about this issue."

He inhaled a large breath and perched on the desk behind him. "There is no need for that, Chief Inspector. Okay, tell me how you think things should progress."

"You should keep the woman under tight surveillance to ensure she doesn't leave the area. I would check the airlines daily to see if she books herself on a flight to the UK. Until she does that, I wouldn't trust a word she says."

"But that could take months. When is Lawrence's court date?"

"Like you say, that is not likely to be for months. If she's still interested in him by then. For all we know, she might find a new wealthy beau in that time."

"So how do you suggest we get around this issue? I cannot keep a man tailing her indefinitely, can I?"

"Let me make some calls back home and see if I can come up with a solution. Give me a couple of hours. Can you keep her here that long in the meantime?"

"I'm sure I can do that. Let me know immediately how you get on." Tiago walked away, running a hand through his thinning hair.

"What are you hatching, Caroline?"

The chief winked at her. "If she's going to be our star witness, I'm sure we can find her some kind of safe house back home. I'd rather have her in our country than out here, given the bloody time it's taken us to obtain the extradition for Lawrence."

"I get it. You're thinking about setting up visiting orders for her to see Lawrence in the nick, too, aren't you? Hoping to obtain further information from both of them once their trust has been gained? You canny cow."

Caroline broke into a broad smile. "Stick with me, girl, and you'll go a long way." She reached for the phone, placed the call to one of her contacts in the witness protection department, and explained the situation. "That's great, Dan. Can you organise that for me? We should be heading back to the UK either today or tomorrow at the latest. I'll give you a ring when we land. I appreciate your help."

Caroline held up her hand, and Miranda high-fived her.

"You're brilliant. Have I ever told you that?" Miranda told her.

"No, but don't stop there. My ego is in dire need of rebuilding after Lawrence's choking session."

Tiago heard them laughing and returned to ask, "Is everything okay?"

"Yes, we're just letting off steam. You'll be pleased to know that we've found an opening for Ms. Estevez in our protection programme. Do you want to deliver the good news or shall I?"

"We should do it together. The three of us."

Miranda nodded and followed Caroline and Tiago into the adjacent room, where Estevez was sitting upright in her chair.

"Good news, Vanessa. I'll let the chief inspector tell you." Tiago smiled and stood back as Caroline sat down opposite the woman.

"What news?" Estevez asked warily.

"You'll be coming back to the UK with us, either later on today or tomorrow. The flight has yet to be finalised."

"I will? For what reason?" The woman spoke perfect English with a heavy accent.

"The sergeant informed me that you are willing to testify against Brad. Is that correct?"

"Yes, if I have to. He's my lover and my friend. It pains me to show such disloyalty towards him, though. If there is another way around this, then that would suit me better."

Caroline frowned at Tiago, who merely shrugged. Turning back to Estevez, she smiled. "I see. I was told otherwise. Yes, we have evidence against Brad that should be enough to convict him. So it's not going to look good that you are so close to this man who likely killed his wife. One might even argue that you were involved or coaxed him to do it." Caroline levelled her with a knowing gaze. "But it would make you look far better in the eyes of the court if you were to testify against Brad. You'll get to speak your piece about how much you love Brad, if you like. Regarding your love affair, he doesn't need to know why you're here, not until the court proceedings, anyhow. But would you really be willing to proceed with a relationship with the man, knowing that he'd killed his wife? Men of this ilk rarely kill only once, in my experience. Would you really be willing to take the risk? One single argument could be enough to trigger his anger at a moment's notice."

"His wife's death was an accident, I…" She trailed off, and her gaze dropped to the desk.

Caroline tried to press her to finish her sentence, but the woman refused. Eventually, the chief gave up. "All right, this is what we're going to do. We'll get someone to take you home, where you'll pack a suitcase with enough for a month or so, nothing too excessive. One case will do. Then we'll put you up in a hotel near the airport."

"Okay, if I must. Where will I stay in the UK, in a hotel?"

"No. We're organising a safe place for you to stay until the court case. It'll be at our expense on the proviso that you live up to your end of the bargain and testify against Brad."

"I agree. Will I still be able to visit him in prison?" Vanessa asked, her eyes welling up with tears.

"Of course, if that's what you want. However, I would strongly advise you not to tell Brad about our agreement."

"Won't he ask why I'm going back to the UK?"

"Probably. We want you to avoid any form of confrontation with him. We've all seen how angry he gets and what occurs when that happens. What harm will it do just to say to him that you are coming to the UK as support for him? We'll play along with you. He won't hear about the agreement from either of us. Will he, Inspector?"

Miranda pretended to zip her mouth shut. "That's a negative from me. Sergeant, you won't let it slip before we leave Portugal, will you?"

"You have my word on that."

"That's sorted then. Sergeant, can you arrange our flights ASAP please?"

"I'll get onto it now. Thank you for your cooperation in this matter, Ms. Estevez."

The woman's lips screwed into a taut smile. "If there is any indication of him knowing the real reason behind my visit, then the deal is off, okay?"

Caroline nodded and rose from her chair. "You have our word on that, Ms. Estevez."

CHAPTER TWELVE

At the airport, Miranda and Caroline sat opposite Lawrence and Estevez in a private area, away from the other passengers. Miranda stared at the loved-up couple in disbelief. She had to force down the bile that had settled in the back of her throat.

Estevez's fingers enclosed Lawrence's cuffed hands, and she smiled at him like a love-struck teenager. Miranda marvelled at the adoration the couple showed one another and wondered what actually went on in the woman's brain. She could certainly never think fondly of—or worse than that, fall in love with—a man who had murdered his wife. *It takes all sorts to live in this strange world of ours. By the looks of things, it's only getting stranger.*

She studied the beautiful woman. Her every eyelash was fixed neatly into position. Her eyebrows were plucked and perfectly shaped like a supermodel's. Her nails, attached to long slender fingers, dripping in gold and diamonds, made Miranda wonder if Estevez had wealth of her own or if she had deliberately latched on to the likes of Lawrence with the intention of spreading her legs for material benefits. That sort of behaviour appeared to be the norm in certain sections of society in this day and age.

Caroline nudged Miranda in the ribs and said out of the corner of her mouth, "What are you thinking?"

"I'm not, really. Just observing the woman and trying to prevent myself from throwing up. Can you believe them? They haven't taken their eyes off each other since we left the station. I could never be that infatuated with a man. Could you?"

Caroline sniggered. "I'm sure Alan would be narked to hear that, love."

"You know what I mean. I love Alan more than I've ever loved any other man, but come on... I'd never fawn over him the way she is. It's bordering on the obscene, isn't it? Or is that me just being a bit callous, given that I know what he's done to his wife?"

Still whispering, Caroline replied, "I suppose it's a bit of both. Don't get me wrong—I'm totally with you on this one. However, it grieves me to say that he does have a certain magnetism that some women would find irresistible."

Miranda turned sharply to look at her. "You're not serious? Christ, maybe you've been single for too long. You need to get laid desperately if you think like that about this murderer."

"Christ, with friends like you…" Caroline paused when one of the flight attendants appeared.

"If you'd like to follow me, you'll be the first to board the plane."

The four of them rose to their feet. Caroline led the group while Miranda brought up the rear. The airline had arranged for the four of them to be seated at the front of the plane, away from the other travellers and close to the attendants' service area in case any problems arose. The middle row contained four seats, allowing the detectives to sit on either side of the suspect and the witness. That also meant Miranda and Caroline would have to endure hours of listening to Lawrence and his girlfriend talking all lovey-dovey to each other and the slurping noises of their wet kisses. That was sure to turn Miranda off the in-flight meal.

An hour into the flight, Lawrence leaned over to Miranda to make his request. "I need the little boy's room."

She sighed heavily. "Can't you wait?"

Lawrence laughed. "Are you volunteering to clean up the mess? Maybe they gave me a dodgy meal at the station last night. I know my guts feel as if they're on fire."

"Really? It's come on that quick? Funny how you never mentioned anything about that before we took off."

Caroline leaned forward. "Everything all right?"

"Yeah, Mr. Wise Guy here reckons his guts are on fire, and he needs the loo."

Caroline grinned broadly. "There's no problem with that. I'll go in with him."

"What? No frigging way, lady. I ain't showing you my bits. I need privacy when I take a shit."

Miranda laughed at his incensed tone. "Take it or leave it, buster."

"You ladies are not being fair to him," Estevez piped up. "What do you expect him to do? Escape out of the window in mid-air?"

The woman had a point, so Miranda reluctantly stood up and allowed Lawrence to pass. She followed him the short distance up the aisle to the small toilet, and with her ear to the door, she waited for him to finish his ablutions and leave the toilet. She cringed when she heard him explode. Pulling her head away, she looked back to see Caroline's shoulders moving up and down as she giggled. *How come I get all the crap jobs? Pun intended!*

Not long after the toilet incident, their meal arrived. Lawrence tried to complain that he was unable to eat properly due to the restraint of his handcuffs, but his whinging was ignored. Even Estevez tried pleading with Caroline and Miranda to unlock the cuffs for a ten minutes' reprieve, but the detectives refused to fall for another of the man's tricks. One near-throttled detective was enough in anyone's book.

The plane landed at Gatwick nearly three hours after it left Lisbon, much to everyone's relief. Miranda had felt especially stifled during the flight. Her backside was numb, and she was dying for actual physical exercise. A bout in the gym wouldn't go amiss later that day. Maybe Caroline would allow her to leave work early. *Fat chance of that happening. I'm bound to have a desk full of crappy paperwork vying for my attention.*

Once they had passed through customs, they located Miranda's car in the car park and drove back to the station. They handed Lawrence over to the duty sergeant, who placed him in a cell, where he would await his transportation to Thameside Prison and be placed on remand. Meanwhile, Vanessa accompanied Miranda to one of the interview rooms. A female constable watched over Vanessa while Miranda chased up Caroline's contact at witness protection. She hoped they had managed to summon up suitable accommodation for their star witness.

As Miranda walked into the incident room, Johnny's expression clearly told her he was both pleased and relieved to see her. "Everything all right, partner?" she asked.

He stood up, approached her, and kissed her on the cheek. Everyone in the room laughed. "I've never, never been so glad to see you in all my life." He pretended to hand her a baton. "Your reins, I believe."

Miranda roared and shook her head. "Good grief, I thought you'd lost your marbles then for a minute."

"Another day, and I think I might have done. At the risk of repeating myself, I don't know how you do it day in and day out. I want to reassure you that I'll *never* try and take over your job. You have my word on that."

Miranda rubbed his arm. "Glad to hear it. Maybe you'll give me a bit of slack now and again from now on when I'm caught up in a foul mood?"

"I wouldn't go that far," Johnny replied, earning himself a slap on the arm.

"Okay, I've only got a few minutes. I need to get the witness settled in her hideaway. Any news?"

"Not really. We're still trying to trace the prints. I chased forensics up this morning, and they told me they thought the results would be imminent."

"I suppose they're running out of prints to check them against by now. It's been that long. Okay, well, there's little we can do about that until we have those results to hand. I'm going to check in with Sheila Morton, apprise her of the situation with Lawrence. We saw the launch party on the local TV out there. She seemed to be holding up well, considering what she's had to contend with in the last week or so."

"Yeah, I caught it, too. It certainly looked that way."

Miranda stopped at the vending machine to buy a much-needed decent cup of coffee then continued into her office. She was surprised to see her desk didn't resemble the aftermath of a bomb explosion. Johnny had done well in her absence, or had he? Fate had an uncanny way of paying her back occasionally. She couldn't help wondering if over the next few weeks, the paperwork he'd completed would somehow find its way back on her desk, requiring substantial corrections. She pushed aside the thought. *He's done his best, which is all I could ask of him.*

She rang Dan, Caroline's contact at the witness protection department, and he confirmed that a small apartment had been set aside for Vanessa's use.

She noted down the address on a slip of paper. "That's great, Dan. Can you arrange for someone to meet me at the location within the hour?"

"I can do that myself, Inspector. I'll see you then."

She ended the call and searched for Sheila's phone number then thought it would be a better idea to call her at the business number instead.

The line rang for several seconds, then a young woman answered.

"Jess, is that you?"

"It is. Who's that?"

"It's DI Miranda Carr. Is Sheila available for a quick chat please?"

"Oh, hi. Yep, she's just finished another call. Hold on a sec."

Beethoven's Fifth filled the line for a few seconds. "Hello, Inspector."

"Hello, Sheila. It's just a quick call to update you on what's been happening the last few days. I hope the launch was successful?"

"It was. The best launch the company has ever had. Jess and I are working sixteen-hour days at present to keep up with the influx of orders. The response has far exceeded even Anneka's forecasted figures."

"Wow, that's excellent news. I'm sorry you're being forced to work the long hours, though. That must be a tremendous strain for both you and your hubby at this sad time. Will you be able to slip back into retirement and hand over the responsibility to someone else soon?"

"I'm not sure I could trust anyone else that much, Inspector. I'm caught between a rock and a hard place at the moment. Jess has been a wonderful source of support to me, though. And James is doing a fabulous job back at the house. He's never had to cook a meal before all this happened, and it's been a very steep learning curve for him, one that he seems to be relishing, for now anyway."

"That all sounds great, Sheila. I hope my news will add to your excitement."

"Oh? Go on, dear?"

"Well, the reason I haven't had a chance to update you on what's been happening is because my DCI and I flew out to Portugal. Umm... we returned earlier today with an unexpected surprise." She smiled at the momentary silence on the other end of the line.

"Surprise, you say?"

"Yes, we brought Brad Lawrence back with us." She heard a thump. "Sheila? Sheila, are you all right?"

"Lord! Yes, I'm fine. I just dropped into my chair. So, you've caught the bastard, have you? Wow, maybe Anneka will get the justice she deserves after all? I feared he would be one of these scoundrels to avoid capture for years. I can't tell you how relieved I am to hear this, Inspector. Thank you for not giving up and for going after the bastard."

"The good news doesn't end there, Sheila."

"Really? Do tell."

A warmth spread through her at the joy she heard in the older woman's voice. "We have a witness who is prepared to testify against Brad. Although that part is very hush-hush right now."

"My goodness. How remarkable. But how? Who? Someone local?"

"Slow down there. Right, her name is Vanessa Estevez—"

"Wait a minute. That name rings a bell."

Miranda's interest piqued, despite her weariness. "That's interesting. If you can recall why, it would help."

"I'm not really sure off the top of my head. Leave that with me a few minutes. Actually, I'm glad you've called. I was going to contact you in the next day or so about a couple of issues that are bothering me."

"Oh, in connection with what?" Miranda had an idea what one of the issues might be—Anneka's funeral. She had no idea why Sheila would need to contact her other than that.

"First of all, we've finally been given the all-clear to bury our daughter. We're hoping to lay her to rest next week. James and I have to go and see the funeral director tomorrow, in fact. Would you like to attend? Is that the done thing even? I have no idea about these things."

"I was going to ask if I could attend. Yes, it is a done thing. I always like to lend my support to the family members burying their loved ones. I'd be honoured to join you. I thought you talked about scattering her ashes before. Have you changed your mind about having a cremation?"

"Yes, in the end, we decided it would be preferable for us to have a place where we could visit Anneka."

"I understand. What was the other reason for you needing to contact me?"

"In between organising the launch, something cropped up with a payment query from one of our suppliers, which made me take a closer look through the accounts for the business. During this time, I had the safe open and noticed Anneka's chequebook inside. There have been some pretty big cheques issued over the last year or so."

"Oh, to whom? Or can I already guess that?"

"Yep, to Brad."

"Do you have the dates? Do they correspond with the dates around the time his business folded?"

"Yes, I'd have to check, but off the top of my head, I think the dates coincide with the collapse of that damn business of his."

"So, he either went cap in hand, begging Anneka for the money, or she gave it to him willingly to help try and salvage his business. I reckon it was probably the latter. From the little I know about your daughter, Sheila, I propose she would have pulled every trick in the book to help Brad's business survive."

"You're very astute, Inspector. She was generous to a fault. Always keen to help others out financially, not that we ever took any of her money, of course. I know she helped out a few of her school friends when they were in strife, nothing major. A few hundred now and again, that's all. The thought of him bleeding her dry really pisses me off. Excuse my language."

"No need to apologise. I can understand that. Please, try not to upset yourself any more than is necessary. He's really not worth you making yourself ill over."

"I know you're right, but I have this awful feeling in the pit of my stomach that he's going to get away with it. You must have similar doubts during cases such as this, Inspector? How do you combat them?"

"Ordinarily, yes. Most of an inspector's day is riddled with doubts. However, I'm urging you not to worry in your daughter's case. This witness will help us slam the door shut on him and ensure the key is never turned to release him. You have my word on that, I swear."

"Thank you, that's reassuring. Estevez you said, right?"

Miranda found herself nodding even though the woman was not in the room with her. "Yes, Vanessa Estevez."

"Vanessa, Vanessa, Vanessa. Well, the only Vanessa I remember Anneka and Brad discussing was a woman they met at a function in Portugal last year, I think. Gosh, I swear my memory some days is truly woeful. Old age is a bugger to contend with."

"Hey, it happens to us all. Look, I'll leave the name with you. Something might crop up when you least expect it. Will you ring me when the funeral details have been finalised?"

"I will. Thanks for letting me know you've got Brad where he belongs—behind bars. That in itself is a load off my mind. James will be over the moon. He's struggled with our loss more than I have. I've had the distraction of the launch to aid my grief. Bless him, James wasn't given that luxury. It's hard being left alone when he usually has me as a permanent fixture beside him day and night. I'm looking into employing a full-time manager for the business soon. I have to, before it starts to take its toll on me. There's a reason I took retirement from the business, and my body is starting to remind me of that fact."

"Take it easy. You'll be no good to anyone if you fall ill, Sheila. All the hard work has been done now. It's time for you to consider easing up. We'll speak soon."

"I'll call the minute we've agreed on the arrangements. Bye for now, and thank you again, Inspector. It feels like the weight of the world has been lifted from my shoulders."

Miranda hung up with a smile. She dialled Alan's number at the office. "Hi, Alan. I'm back on English soil again."

"Whew... what a relief. Are you at the station or at home?"

"Still at work. I have a few loose ends to tie up here first. I should be home around sixish. Shall I pick up a takeaway on the way home?"

"Why not? It's been a while since we've stretched to one of those. Are you all right? You sound knackered."

"I'm fine. That's the relief showing in my voice. It's great to have the culprit locked up behind bars. I just have to settle someone into a flat before I sign off for the night, and then I'll head straight home, I promise."

"Sounds ominous. Dare I ask what that cryptic message means?"

"No, don't ask. I'll tell you all about it later."

"All right. See you soon. Oh, and Miranda... I've missed you loads. It's been like half of me has been missing. I've only been able to work at fifty per cent capacity."

"I've missed you, too, sweetie. We'll make up for the lost time when I get home and over the weekend, I promise."

"I'll hold you to that and look forward to it. Love you."

She was too busy smiling and didn't even notice he'd hung up until she heard the line-dead tone.

CHAPTER THIRTEEN

Miranda's Friday morning started off with a staff meeting. Even the chief was there to join in the fun. "Right, well, from now on I think we should be chasing evidence, such as the prints on the knife. Johnny, will you get on to that again for me this morning?"

"Yep, first call after the meeting."

"Good. We need to look at anything and everything now, start building a water-tight case to ensure Brad goes down and isn't set free on a technicality, all right?"

"Have you checked on Vanessa recently?" Caroline asked.

"I thought I'd go out there after the chore of morning paperwork was completed. Any particular reason you asked?"

"Nope, just asking."

Miranda frowned, aware that the chief never asked a question just for the sake of having something to say. Miranda made a mental note to tackle her about the subject after the meeting then said, "I think we should be concentrating most of our energy on trying to find out the motive behind Lawrence killing his wife."

"Money?" Craig offered with a shrug.

"Boredom? Keen to end the marriage and move on to the next unsuspecting victim?" Lindsey threw in.

As the team shouted their responses, Miranda wrote on the incident board and circled each answer before writing down the next. "Good. Come on, people. Keep them coming."

"That's enough right there, isn't it?" Johnny asked. "Why do most people kill their spouses? Either to get the insurance money, inherit a large sum after a victim is popped off, or to start afresh with someone new."

"If you take all that into consideration, then it looks like all those scenarios could be contributing factors in this case. Good point about the insurance. Will you look into that side of things for me, Lindsey? Also, I think it'll be worth ringing Anneka's solicitor to see when the will is due to be read. Maybe that will give us a clearer indication of what was going on in Anneka's head. Perhaps she suspected Brad of having an affair and threatened to cut him out of the will. Who knows? Lindsey, get in touch with the solicitor. Let's see if she enquired about making any alterations."

Lindsey jotted down the request in her notebook. "Okay."

"Anything else?" Miranda asked, more out of hope than expectation.

The team shook their heads in response.

"Very well then, let's get back to work and dig, dig, dig, guys."

She walked past Caroline. "Care for a coffee in my office, boss?"

"I don't mind if I do. Thank you kindly."

The two women bought a coffee from the machine and stepped into the office.

"Spit it out," Miranda demanded once the office door was closed behind them.

"What? I'm not sure what you're getting at."

"Why did you ask if I had visited the witness?"

Caroline hitched up her right shoulder. "Simple question."

"Do you think she's going to do a runner?"

"The thought had occurred to me. Don't tell me you haven't thought the same."

"It's only been a few days since she arrived. That reminds me, I must ring the prison to see if she's arranged a visit yet. Do you think the warden will give us special dispensation to allow her to visit more frequently? You know, if we tell him what we're hoping to achieve?" Miranda asked. She blew on her coffee before taking a sip.

"You can try. We need to be cautious. We can't go taping their conversations. You're aware of that, yes?"

"I know, but we can call the guards as witnesses when the court case comes around, can't we? I'll ask the warden, see if his men will take special note of the conversations. I'm sure Brad and Vanessa will be careful of what they say in front of strangers, but one slip of the tongue could spell history for either or both of them."

"All right, I'll allow that. One whiff of entrapment, though, and the defence will be on us in a shot."

Miranda tutted. "I ain't new to this game, Chief, in case you hadn't noticed."

Johnny knocked then barged in without being invited, his eyes as large as saucers. "Boss, we've got a match on the print."

Caroline swivelled in her chair to look at him. "Who? Tell us, for Christ's sake, man."

"Who is it, Johnny?"

He flopped into the spare chair. "Estevez."

"That's great. Then we should go round there and arrest her immediately. Star witness status or not. She's not going to get out of this one now, not when we have her at the scene," Miranda said, excitement causing her to spill some of her coffee. She frowned when Johnny put his hand up to prevent her from saying anything further.

"You need to rein in your excitement for a moment, boss."

"Get on with it, man!" Caroline urged, glaring at Johnny.

"Stop toying with us, Johnny. You said it was Estevez. What gives?"

"Yes, it's Estevez—that part is true—just not Vanessa Estevez."

"What the fuck? Who then?"

"Luis Estevez," Johnny told them, fanning the flames of frustration.

"Who in God's name is that? A brother? A husband? Father? Who?" Miranda flung herself back in her chair. *Why is nothing ever simple?*

Caroline ran a hand over her face. "That's incredible. How? Why didn't either of them say anything? Is that why Vanessa wanted to come back here? Is this relative still in the UK?"

Miranda clicked her fingers and pushed out of her chair. "We're wasting time. Let's get over there to see what she has to say about this."

Caroline stared up at her. "I'd take a breath before I stormed over there if I were you, Miranda."

She plonked down in her chair again. "What do you suggest doing then? Let her roam free, so she can tip him off? Whoever *he* is."

"No, not in the slightest. Just think things over thoroughly. Carry out all the checks you need to do, go in there fully armed with information. You know the drill, Miranda."

"Yeah, I do. I just thought it would be better to get over there and question her before she gets fidgety or she and this Luis decide to make a run for it. Johnny, check with the airport immigration. See if they have any knowledge of this Estevez arriving. If they do, I want to know when. Jesus, I can't believe I missed this. I knew there was no way on earth a heavy rug with Anneka's body rolled up inside could be shifted by Brad and Vanessa."

"There you go again. Stop blaming yourself. How could we have known without the forensics to show us the way?" Caroline tried to reassure her as Johnny left the room.

"I still think we need to get over there ASAP, Caroline."

"Fair enough, but not before you're armed and dangerous, girl. The plot thickens, eh?"

"And some. Look, I've got to get on. Sorry to be so rude."

Caroline stood up and held out her hand for Miranda to high-five. "Promise me you won't get down about this? Look on it as a positive, all right? The more ammunition you collect to hit them with, the better, okay?"

"All right. I'll ring you later when we know anything solid."

For the next hour, the team frantically searched everywhere available to them for information on the male Estevez. However, nothing at all presented itself. Miranda kicked out in frustration and sent a chair flying across the room. "Why? Why can't we find anything? Right, never mind. Johnny, get your jacket on. We're going to see our valuable witness."

In the car, Johnny eyed her warily.

"You can talk. I'm not about to snap your head off."

"Really? I'll chance it then. How are you going to play it when we get there?"

"By ear. I don't want to go in there screaming and shouting. I'd rather not let on that we know about her relative from the outset. Damn, I'm not sure I'm going to be able to contain myself when I get there. Neither contain, nor control. I just want to haul her arse in and leave her stewing in a bloody cell for a week as punishment. Bitch!"

"Calm down, boss. Going in there in that frame of mind isn't going to get you very far. We need to keep her on side, don't we?"

"Yeah, I know that, Johnny. I'm just using the journey over there to vent. I'll be calmer once we get there, I promise. And for your information, I don't need reminding that we need to keep her on our side." She smiled tightly at him.

He had the decency to look embarrassed by his faux pas. "Sorry."

They pulled into a small parking space just around the corner from the flat where Vanessa was staying. Miranda had already instructed the woman not to open the door to anyone who could not provide the coded message: three rings, a pause then another three rings on the bell. The woman seemed surprised to see the two detectives when she opened the door wearing a tiger-print onesie.

"Hi, Vanessa. Mind if we come in? We were in the area." Miranda beamed at the woman, who pushed the door open wide to let them in.

"I'm surprised to see you, Inspector. I was still in bed. Is something wrong?"

"No, like I said, we were in the area. Have you settled in okay?"

"Yes. Very well, thank you."

"Good. Have the neighbours welcomed you, or have you had any other visitors lately?" Miranda cursed herself for asking the question before making the woman feel at ease to gain her confidence.

"It's only been a few days, Inspector. I won't be expecting any visitors in the near future. Not unless you let Brad out on a day-release pass."

Miranda scoffed. "Not going to happen in my lifetime, Ms. Estevez. Any chance of a cup of coffee?"

"Very well, come through and make yourself at home. That is what you Brits say, isn't it?" she asked, trying out her upper-class British accent.

"Yes, that's right on the button. Well done." Through narrowed eyes, Miranda watched Estevez move around the small flat. She decided it would be better to set a smile in place in case the woman unexpectedly turned to look at her. Once the coffee was made, the three of them took a seat at the rickety kitchen table. "How are you liking it here, Vanessa?"

"All right, I suppose."

"Have you heard when you'll be able to visit Brad yet?"

"No. I thought that sort of news would come from you. I have no idea how to go about arranging something like that." Estevez looked panic-stricken at the thought of having to deal with the authorities at the prison herself.

"I'll see what I can do. I was going to ring the warden today to see if Brad was behaving himself anyway. I'll get back to you about a visit this afternoon. I can't see there being a problem. What did your parents say about you being in London for the next month or two? They'll miss you, I would imagine." Miranda attempted to tease the information about her relatives out of her, all the time keeping her smile firmly fixed in place.

"That would be super. I'm dying to see him. I know we only saw each other yesterday, but when you are two people in love as much as we are, any time apart is devastating. My father died years ago, waste of space he was. Vile, abusive man. Even my mother cried with relief the day he died. My mother is starting to slow down now. I do my best for her, help out paying the bills, et cetera, but it does become a strain now and again."

Is that why you latched onto Brad? Only, he wasn't the one with the money in his bank account, was he? "You have to carry the burden of looking after your mum yourself then? No siblings to help you out?"

"No. Just me and dear old Mum. She's only sixty-five. There are distant relatives dotted around Portugal, but no one I intend to invite in my home to snoop around. We fell out with the rest of the family years ago when Mum refused to leave Dad. His abusive nature shone like a beacon. Everyone except dear old Mum could see what he was like. His threats frightened the rest of the family. Instead of sticking by my mother, lending her some support, they cut us out of their lives. I won't break down and beg them for help now. Mum has good neighbours who will look after her during my trip here. I have a far greater need to be by Brad's side."

Miranda's mind worked overtime whilst the woman spoke. Her lack of eye contact was a telling sign that Miranda should take the woman's story with a pinch of salt. Something about the woman didn't ring true. However, despite wracking her brains, she couldn't figure out what.

"It's always nice to have good neighbours you can trust not to take advantage of a situation."

That got Vanessa's attention. She stared at Miranda for a few seconds before responding. "Yes, I trust them to care for my mother as well as I could. Tell me, Inspector, why do you have a sudden interest in my family members?"

"I'm sorry if I seemed intrusive, Vanessa. I'm just trying to ensure your visit goes smoothly. Distractions back at home could prove detrimental to your stay with us. God forbid anything should happen to your mother in your absence. I just wanted to make sure that all was well back at home for the foreseeable future. No need to be alarmed. I'm simply covering all the bases."

"I see. Then I apologise for my outburst."

"You're allowed to be a little tetchy, given the circumstances. It's just a shame that you don't have any family members around you in the UK to be of comfort to you in the coming months." That would be the final time she would mention the family. The last thing she wanted to do was highlight the idea that they were aware of Luis Estevez.

"No. No family over here. The only family I have in the UK is sitting in a prison cell right now. Would you mind making the call to try and arrange a visit at the prison?"

Miranda's smile broadened, and she withdrew her mobile from her jacket pocket. "Of course. I'll go outside. The reception doesn't appear to be too good in here."

Miranda left Johnny in the flat with Vanessa while she placed the call she had tried to make at the station before setting out, only to be told that the warden was in a staff meeting.

Finally, the warden accepted her call, and they came to a compromise. He said he would be willing to let Brad Lawrence have regular visits if he felt it would help Miranda's case. He even said that he would guarantee one of his most trusted officers was stationed in the room during the visit, suggesting that officer would relay any useful information he overheard during the visit. After booking a visit for that afternoon at four, Miranda returned to the flat.

"It obviously helps to have contacts in high places. You have a visit arranged for this afternoon at four, Vanessa."

The woman left her chair and flung her arms excitedly around Miranda. "Thank you, thank you, thank you! How wonderful you are to be treating Brad and me so well... after all that has happened."

"I'll arrange for a taxi to pick you up around three thirty, how's that?"

"Wonderful. That leaves me four hours to look my best for him."

"We'll take our leave now then. Good luck this afternoon. It's always a pleasure going the extra mile for someone willing to testify against a murderer."

Her words were meant as a stark reminder to the woman in case, in her loved-up state, she had forgotten her side of the bargain.

During the ride back to the station, Johnny kept shaking his head.

"What's wrong?" Miranda eventually asked when she pulled up at a red light.

"I just don't get it."

"What? At least give me a clue, partner?"

"If she has no relatives in the UK and no male relatives that she's in touch with back in Portugal, then who is this Luis Estevez geezer?"

Miranda shrugged. The question had been floating around her mind, as well. "I'm at a loss on that one, too. You checked with immigration, and they couldn't shed any light, either. So what gives? Unless…"

"Go on?"

"Unless it's a coincidence. What if Estevez is a common name out there? Like Smith is in the UK, at least it used to be. We haven't even considered that, have we?"

"Immigration check came back blank, remember? Yeah, too much of a coincidence to me, that one. I'm still inclined to think she's lying about her relatives. Don't tell me you didn't notice the lack of eye contact when she was telling us her sob story?"

"You're right. I had noticed." She slammed the heel of her hand onto the steering wheel and sounded the horn by mistake. "Shit! Sorry," she mouthed to the driver of the car in front. "Shit, damn, and blast! What the fuck are we missing, Johnny?"

"I don't know. Hey, did you notice the pills on the side in the kitchen?"

Miranda turned her head sharply to look at him. "No, can't say I did. What do you suppose they're for? She looks fit enough to me."

"I don't know, I'm not psychic! Hey, you should be praising me for my powers of observation."

She patted his knee. "Good job, young man. I would be praising you more if you'd got the name of the medication she was on. Shit happens, though, right?"

"I knew there'd be a negative attached to the praise. There always is," Johnny grumbled.

Miranda put the car into gear and pulled away, wondering what kind of medication Vanessa Estevez was on. Maybe she had a heart problem or something serious along those lines. If she did, she hid the symptoms well. Miranda made a mental note to ring Tiago when she got back to her office.

CHAPTER FOURTEEN

Miranda's afternoon proved to be surprisingly busy. She told Johnny to be ready to leave at three fifteen, as she intended to be at the prison overseeing Vanessa's visit with Brad. In the meantime, she rang Tiago. Unfortunately, he was on leave until the following Monday and couldn't return her call until then. The next thing on her to-do list was to ring Sheila, who had left a message for Miranda to contact her regarding the funeral. A quick call to Anneka's mother confirmed that the service would be held at eleven on Monday morning. *Damn, another busy day ahead of me then!*

By the time she and Johnny left the station that afternoon, she felt physically and mentally exhausted. "Boy, am I looking forward to putting my feet up this weekend."

"Are you doing anything special?"

"Well, Alan and I were supposed to be going away for the weekend to a country hotel, but I think we're going to have to put those plans on hold. Mum called an emergency meeting about the flower arrangements."

"Crap! See? I told you the better option would have been to elope. Who has the time to deal with weddings when you work full-time?"

"Hey, don't I know it. I think Mum has got everything worked out now. It's just colours she's keen to discuss."

"Mind if we change the subject? Wedding talk freaks me out the more anniversaries Francis and I celebrate. I can't help feeling pressured into popping *the* question. It's all she's talking about at home at the moment, what with yours and a friend of hers weddings being just around the corner."

"Poor thing. Hey, no one should ever feel pressured into doing something against their will, love. Stand firm on that. You hear me?"

"Yeah, for what it's worth. You know Francis—once she's got her heart set on something, there's no restraining her."

"Sounds like you two need to sit down and have a serious chat before things get out of hand."

Johnny shuddered. "Not keen on that choice. Me and sitting down for a chat aren't suitably compatible really."

"You are funny. You always brighten my darkest hours."

They arrived at the prison with half an hour to spare. The warden had set aside a few minutes so they could fill him in on their intentions.

George Watkins listened with his hands together and his steepled forefingers touching his chin. "Like I said on the phone, Inspector, I will put one of my best men inside the visiting room, and I've also arranged for you to observe the interactions between the couple in an adjacent room, although you won't be able to hear what's going on. It's the best I can do for you, I'm afraid."

"I appreciate any help you can give us. We have proof of another suspect involved in the crime, but we're having trouble tracking that person down at the moment. We're hoping Brad or Vanessa will make the mistake of telling us where that person is hiding out. If we can't gather the information we need, then I'm going to make damn sure the judge is aware of the situation. Hopefully, it'll lead to Lawrence's downfall. The judge might even hand out a harsher sentence. We live in hopes, anyway."

"The woman is a witness for you, didn't you say?" Watkins frowned.

"Yes, that's correct. It's a tricky situation because we have DNA pointing to a relative of hers, or at least someone with the same surname."

"Hmm... that's pretty perplexing and frustrating, I should imagine."

"It is. We're keeping a careful eye on the flat where she's staying just in case she has any visitors, but I think the odds on this 'relative' ever turning up again are minimal, especially now the dirty deed has already been dealt with."

"Then let's hope you manage to obtain the information you're seeking through her visits to the prisoner. Shall we make our way down to the observation room? Time's getting on."

Miranda and Johnny followed the warden through the corridors to a small square room that had a TV monitor and recording equipment sitting on a desk along one wall.

In the end, to everyone's disappointment, the couple made every effort not to do anything out of the ordinary. When the meeting finished, the officer who had overseen the meeting joined the detectives and the warden. He reported that Brad and Vanessa had conducted the meeting in a very 'cagey manner.'

Miranda and Johnny headed back to the station. "Crap! Right, we've got to put this source of frustration out of our minds for the weekend. We can't do anything about it. What is concerning me is what type of drugs Vanessa is on."

"In what respect?"

"What if she's on medication for depression? What if she tries to top herself before the case gets to court?"

Johnny shook his head. "You're overthinking this, boss. There's no way that woman is likely to take an overdose. She's too in love with him."

"Yeah, but take that a little further. What if two or three weeks down the line she spirals into a deep depression? Apart from her visits to see him, my guess is she's going to be spending every hour of the day locked up in that flat. That's going to feel like she's living in a prison herself, isn't it? All I'm saying is that if she's on medication for depression, we need to be aware that things could go awry at the flick of a switch. Maybe not now, but…"

"I hear you. Damn, if only the print wasn't so small on those pill pots."

"Yeah, if only. Roll on Monday, eh?"

After spending a relaxing weekend with Alan—pigging out and snuggled up in front of the TV, watching back-to-back episodes of *Blacklist* on Saturday then sorting out the final wedding plans with her parents on Sunday—Miranda was back to work as usual on Monday at eight thirty.

The first call she made was to Portugal. Because they were an hour ahead, she assumed Tiago would already be at work. However, he'd been delayed on a flight back from America. Miranda left a message, reiterating the urgency. Again, she was assured that Tiago would ring her as soon as he turned up for duty.

To avoid letting her frustration fester, Miranda sorted through her post for a couple of hours.

At ten thirty, Johnny poked his head around the door to remind her of the time. "Are you ready to go? We don't want to be late."

Miranda smiled. "Yep, I'm good to go. Let me nip to the loo first, and I'll meet you in the car park, okay?"

"Too much info, boss. Thanks for conjuring up that image."

"Get out, saddo. It's called nature."

Miranda topped up her lipstick and ran a comb through her hair. *Let's get this out of the way. It's sure to be a sad affair. Stiff upper lip, come on, girl. You can do this.*

She straightened the collar on her white blouse and smoothed out the creases in her black skirt and jacket. Then she rushed down the stairs to find her partner leaning impatiently against the bonnet of the car. "Don't say it. Just get in and keep your smart-mouth comments to yourself, for a change."

He shrugged. "That's where you're wrong. I wasn't about to say anything at all, except time's moving on. We'll be lucky if we get there before the service starts at this rate."

"That's all right. We have a secret weapon at hand, don't forget."

After a couple of minutes of driving, Miranda instructed her partner to attach the light and hit the siren. They arrived at the church with seconds to spare. "Crap, look at all the press here."

"What did you expect? She was a celebrity. It kind of comes with the territory."

They stepped out of the car and joined the line of mourners just making their way into church. One of the reporters Miranda knew well called out to her for a statement. She glared at him, forcing home the point that this was neither the time nor the place for his questions.

"Have some respect, Rod," she uttered to the offending reporter.

His cheeks coloured up, and he gave a brief, apologetic nod before retreating into the press pack.

Sheila and James shook hands with Miranda and Johnny at the entrance to the church.

"Thank you for attending, both of you. It means so much to James and me that you should be here," Sheila said, her already-red, sore-looking eyes misting up.

"It's not a problem. We're sorry for your loss and glad the culprit is behind bars, where he belongs."

"It certainly helps knowing that is indeed the case, Inspector. We're so grateful for the time and effort your team have put into the case. We'll be forever grateful to you all," James added, his own eyes brimming with tears.

Miranda and Johnny smiled and continued into the church. All the pews were almost full, but they managed to find a spot at the back behind one of the huge stone pillars. The service was beautiful. Anneka's parents had opted for traditional music to be played as the coffin made its way down the aisle, with Anneka's father acting as the lead pallbearer. A number of Anneka's friends read personal eulogies to their dearly departed friend. Miranda could tell the young woman, in spite of her wealth and notoriety, had held on to her friends for years, since her schooldays, judging by some of the eulogies. Miranda struggled to maintain her professionalism and succumbed to shedding a few tears of sadness on a couple of occasions.

Once the service and the burial had finished, Miranda and Johnny made their excuses and drove back to work. "Very sad," she mumbled under her breath more than once during the journey.

They pushed through the doors to the incident room, where they received mixed reactions.

The atmosphere in the room foxed even the astute Miranda Carr. "What's going on, guys?"

"You might want to hear that in your office, Inspector. You, too, Sergeant. Make it snappy."

Miranda looked in the direction of her office doorway and saw the chief standing there, her expression scarier than one belonging to a character in a Stephen King movie about to slay her victim. The chief turned her back on them and disappeared into the office.

"Oh, crap! What the hell have I done wrong now?" she whispered to Johnny, pulling at the sleeve of his jacket. "I'm glad I'm not going to face her wrath on my own. We better get in there and see what's eating her."

"Close the door behind you," Caroline ordered. She was leaning against the wall, her arms folded, staring out the window.

"Chief? Has something happened?"

"You could say that. Take a seat, both of you. The news I have to deliver will knock you off your feet."

Miranda and Johnny exchanged worried glances. When they were both seated on either side of Miranda's desk, Caroline stood between them, her eyes focused on Miranda as she delivered the news.

"While you were attending the victim's funeral, I learnt something interesting, very interesting, about the murderers," Caroline said with a glint in her eye.

"Like what? You've heard where this Luis Estevez is?" Miranda asked, hope trickling through her veins.

"In a way, yes." The chief stared at her for a long time.

"I can't even begin to imagine what you're about to tell me. It's obviously something really bad, judging by the serious expression on your face. Please, just tell us?"

"Our friend Tiago tried to contact you. As you weren't around, his call was put through to me."

"Okay, so he's obviously found out something integral to the case about Estevez."

"Not what you're thinking. That's for sure. He did as you asked and telephoned Vanessa's doctor with regard to the medicine she is taking. Eventually, the doctor dished out the truth." The chief paused again, and Miranda tutted, voicing her frustration. "Patience, dear friend. Hold on to your hats—here comes the good part. Vanessa and Luis are…" Caroline paused, milking her part.

"Caroline! For God's sake! *Tell us!*"

"One and the same person," the chief said.

"What? What are you talking about? She's in disguise. Is that what you mean?"

"No, Vanessa is transgender. On the change."

"What the fuck? Really? This is you just playing silly buggers with us, isn't it?" Miranda's eyes almost popped out onto the desk when Caroline slowly shook her head.

"Nope. One hundred per cent bang on the mark the truth. It explains a lot if you sit back and think about it, Miranda."

She ran a hand through her hair, tugging at a knot the slight breeze at the funeral had fixed there. "Jesus, that's just weird, isn't it?"

"In what way? To each their own, I say."

"Not that she's chosen to go down that route. I hear it takes a hell of a lot of courage to go through such a major operation. No, the fact that Lawrence and Vanessa are an item. Shit! Do you think he even knows?"

"That's the first thought that occurred to me. My take on it is that he's clueless."

"Shit, damn, and blast. So, *she* was there at the scene when he killed Anneka. Or did Vanessa do it alone? Do we have the wrong person in prison? He keeps telling us Anneka's death was an accident. Holy crap! Why the fuck hasn't he dobbed her in? He doesn't look the type to take the rap for others. Jesus, I really can't get my head around this. Johnny, are you all right?"

All the colour had drained from her partner's face, and his mouth was gaping open. He shook his head, clamped his mouth shut, and nodded.

Amused, the chief said, "Why don't you go and get us all a coffee, Johnny? You look as though you need one."

Stunned, Johnny left the room.

"What do you think we should do now?" the chief asked.

"Arrest her. What else can we do?" Miranda replied.

Johnny returned with three cups of strong black coffee, placed them on the desk, and returned to his seat.

"Okay, that's what I was leading up to. I'd like to be there when you arrest the bitch. Johnny, you stay here, all right?"

"Suits me. Shit, you just couldn't make this crap up, could you? Oh God, the thought of it. Christ knows how Brad Lawrence is going to react. I find it hard to believe he doesn't know." Johnny said, scratching his head at the thought.

"There's only one way to find out," Miranda told him.

"Hold up there, Miranda. I'm thinking we go and arrest Vanessa, then we swing by the prison to see Lawrence. Of course I have no intention of telling him what we've discovered. Let's just see how he reacts to the news that Vanessa has been arrested and go from there."

"You're an evil woman, Caroline."

The chief shrugged, a smirk developing on her face. "That'll teach the bastard not to mess with me. He'll regret trying to throttle the life out of me. Ah, karma, what a wonderful thing."

CHAPTER FIFTEEN

Miranda drove Caroline to Vanessa's flat.

"Before we get there, have you even mentioned the name Luis to her? Intimating that we know he was at the scene or involved in the case?" Caroline asked.

Miranda pulled into the car park near the flat and parked the car. "What kind of detective do you take me for? Since when do I show all my hands to a suspect?"

"All right, simple question. I'm dying to see her face."

"I don't suppose Tiago supplied you with the name of the drugs she's on, did he?"

"Yep, I forgot to tell you. I have them written down on a piece of paper here."

Miranda nodded. "Great, we'll match them up, just to make sure. I wonder what type of drugs they are. Some kind of hormone, do you think?"

"He said something about them being fat redistributing drugs, androgen blockers—whatever they are—and oestrogen. The thought of having to pop pills for the rest of my life wouldn't exactly fill me with glee, I can tell you," Caroline said, screwing up her nose.

"I'm with you on that one. What happens if she stops taking them?"

They left the car and started up the stairs to the flat. "I dread to think. She'll become hairy again, I should imagine. Hey, don't ask me. I ain't an expert in this field."

Miranda laughed. "Maybe we should find one and ask them the question. This is it."

She rang the coded message on the flat's bell. Vanessa, fully clothed this time, held open the door, looking perplexed. The chief marched inside, not giving the woman either the time to ask what they were doing there or to close the door in their faces.

Miranda grinned as she passed the shocked woman. "Hello again, Vanessa."

The woman mumbled something in Portuguese under her breath and then closed the door behind the officers.

"Inspector? Did you forget something the other day?"

"We just wanted to make sure your visit at the prison went okay, Vanessa."

The woman's gaze drifted between the detectives. "Really? You didn't mention that you would be back to see me after the visit. Is this normal? Do you not trust me? Is that the case, Inspector?"

The chief replied before Miranda had a chance to open her mouth. "No, it's not normal. But then, this case is anything but normal, in more ways than one, Vanessa."

"I don't understand. Oh, yes... because of the extradition, of course."

Miranda smiled. "That and other things. Do you mind if we ask you a few questions?"

"No, take a seat."

The three women sat at the kitchen table, and Vanessa continued to eye the detectives warily.

"Something has come up in our investigation that we need your help with, Vanessa."

"What is that, Inspector?"

"When my partner and I visited you the other day, you informed us that you had no family members here in the UK. You even went further to tell us that you no longer had any *male* family members in Portugal, either. Is that correct?"

"Yes, that is correct. Why?"

Miranda went on to ask, "Well, evidence has been discovered which seems to doubt what you told us."

"I don't understand. Please tell me where this is going, Inspector."

Miranda glanced at Caroline, who winked at her, urging her on. Then the chief rose from the table and walked across the room. Miranda had a notion what Caroline was about to do and tried to distract the suspect with another query. "Tell me, Vanessa, does the name Luis mean anything to you?"

The woman's façade faltered briefly, but she quickly recovered and tilted her head. "It is a very popular name in my country, Inspector. Why do you ask?"

Miranda pinned one of her toothy smiles in place. "I'm sure it is. However, we have evidence to suggest that a Luis Estevez was at the Lawrence residence on the night of Anneka's murder."

The woman's eyes dropped to the table, and she began wringing her hands nervously. Miranda prepared herself to pounce on the woman, given her past record of taking flight when cornered. Caroline returned and placed the medication tubs on the table, directly where Vanessa was staring. The woman remained silent for a good few seconds, so Caroline prompted her for a response.

"When did you have the operation, Vanessa?"

"Last year. Oh my God. I can't believe you found out. Please, he doesn't know."

Miranda shook her head. "What? Brad has no knowledge of the operation? No knowledge of Luis's existence?"

"No, I beg of you, please do not tell him. I love him. He loves me. That's all that should matter, surely."

"How misguided can you be? Was Anneka just an inconvenience then? Is that why you two killed her? Because she got in the way?"

"No, I swear, it was an accident."

Miranda slapped the table, scaring the woman into making eye contact with her. "It was an accident to sink a long-bladed knife into her chest? Please, you'll have to enlighten me on how something like that can occur."

"No. That was Brad—he did that. Our intention was just to scare her a little. That's all. Things got out of hand."

"No shit, Sherlock!" Caroline heaved a long sigh. "What possessed you to take her life like that? Brad could have divorced her and run off with you, if that's what you both wanted. Why end Anneka's life?"

Vanessa's gaze dropped back to the table. "He asked her for more money, and she refused."

"For his business, you mean?" Miranda asked.

"No, just money to live on. He struggled to find anyone to invest in his business, so he expected money from her. He said she owed him."

"For *what*? Putting up with his wandering eye?" Caroline snapped back.

"No. He only had eyes for me, not other women."

"So he told you. What if we could prove differently? Would you even listen to us, or are you so caught up in this man that you believe his lies?" Miranda asked, bluffing. They had no idea if Brad had been involved with other women. She was angry that two people could possibly conceive ending a life the way they had and show little remorse for their disgusting behaviour.

Vanessa looked horrified at the suggestion that her beloved had been with women other than her. "No, he wouldn't do that to me. I don't believe you." Tears tumbled down her cheeks.

"You cry tears over the thought of him playing away, and yet you show nothing—no remorse or guilt—for taking an innocent woman's life. What kind of person are you?"

Through her sobs, she said pitifully, "Someone who is crying out to be loved. Is that so wrong, Inspector?"

Miranda launched out of her chair and withdrew the cuffs from her pocket. "You disgust me. All this has been about what you and Brad want, and you'll screw anyone who got in the way. That's it, isn't it? You're selfish, plain and simple. Get up!"

Caroline took up position next to Vanessa, as if to prevent her striking Miranda, but the suspect seemed too dumbstruck even to contemplate lashing out. She stood slowly and placed her hands behind her back, ready for Miranda to slap on the cuffs.

Caroline picked up the medication and popped them in her handbag.

"Leave them. They are no use to me, not today, not ever, if you lock me up," Vanessa said, her voice sounding strained.

They returned to the station, where a sorrowful-looking Vanessa was read her rights and banged up in a cell.

Before they knocked off duty for the night, Miranda and Caroline visited Brad in prison. He seemed amused, if a little surprised, to see them again so soon after returning from Portugal.

"Well, well, well, ladies. May I ask what brings you to pay me a visit? Do you have a court hearing date, perhaps?"

Miranda let Caroline take charge of the meeting. "No. That should be through any day now. We're here to inform you that you won't have to go through the ordeal alone."

He frowned and narrowed his eyes. "I'm not with you."

"Then I'll clarify things for you, Mr. Lawrence. Today, we had the pleasure of arresting your accomplice in your wife's murder."

His lip curled up at the side. "I didn't have an accomplice, and I've already told you my wife's death was an accident, not *murder*."

Caroline winked at Brad. "That's not what Vanessa is saying. It's a shame you guys won't be able to collaborate anymore to make sure your story is tighter than a baboon's arse."

Brad lunged across the desk, but the guard standing behind him grabbed his shoulders and forced him back into his chair.

Caroline and Miranda stood and made their way to the door, then Caroline threw back at him, "Have a nice life, Brad. Too bad your parents didn't teach you crime doesn't pay."

"You can't prove a thing. Anneka's death was an accident," he shouted after them as they left the room.

Caroline and Miranda high-fived each other as they walked up the corridor. "Yeah and we'll have pleasure proving otherwise in court, mate. Hold on to your hat. You're in for the effing ride of your life," Caroline said, chuckling.

EPILOGUE

Miranda and Alan's wedding ended up being a perfect day. Her parents did them proud with the flowers, which meant extra orders for the nursery that was now up and running again.

Married life was everything Miranda and Alan hoped it would be, and their beautiful honeymoon to the Maldives was a wonderful memory caught on film that would live forever in their minds and hearts.

A few months later, Miranda was back to reality, and the day of Brad Lawrence's court case descended on a crisp October morning. Miranda stopped off at work long enough to set the rest of the team their tasks for the day—the latest murder enquiry to land on the desk was of a teenager caught up in a sex-ring case. Then she dropped by Caroline's office. "Can I go through?" she asked the chief's secretary.

"Go on. She's expecting you. Good luck with the case today. I hope the pair of them get banged up for life."

"Yep, I'm optimistic all the evidence we've put forward will see that hope come to fruition, Cindy."

Caroline was just slipping on her navy jacket when Miranda opened the door. "Are you ready to roll?" Miranda asked her friend.

"Let's go get him, or should I say them? Christ, I'm so looking forward to this day. I want to get an early seat. No dilly-dallying on the way. You hear me?"

"Calm down. We've got plenty of time on our hands."

They found a courtroom seat with a good view of the defendants. The room soon filled up with members of the public, and just like at Anneka's funeral, the press swarmed in.

Miranda nodded to Brad when the cocksure individual made his way into the defendant's box. His arrogance beamed like a ray of light from a lighthouse, guiding the judge to a conviction as if he were a ship in a storm.

Caroline nudged Miranda when the door opened again. "Here we go, let the good times roll."

Miranda didn't know where to look first—at Brad, emanating his overconfidence, or at the person whose footsteps were slowly ascending the steps. "Look at his face. The effing penny ain't dropped yet."

Brad glanced at the bearded new arrival and threw his chin up in the air, turning his head to the side. Miranda watched the other defendant take his seat, and she stifled a grin. "Jesus, what a difference, no wonder he hasn't got a clue."

"All rise. The right honourable Judge Elizabeth Barrett residing," the court usher's voice boomed out, silencing the crowd.

Miranda sensed the anxiety coming from the defendant's counsel's bench as each of them turned to face the two defendants. The thought crossed her mind that Brad probably thought the other defendant was there on another charge. Maybe he wasn't familiar with the workings of a high court.

The bailiff watched the judge take her seat before he carried on with his duty. He announced the case number, Brad's name in full, and the name of the other defendant: Luis Estevez. That grabbed Brad's attention. He turned sharply to face the person.

Estevez reached out with cuffed hands and pleaded with Brad, "I'm sorry, my love. Please forgive me?"

Brad struggled with what to do next. He got to his feet, but the court officer standing behind him ordered him to sit down. Then under every gaze in the courtroom, he bent over, and the whole courtroom could hear him throwing up.

Estevez looked devastated by Brad's reaction and tried again to beg for mercy.

After a few seconds of spilling his guts, Brad sat up and wiped his mouth on the back of his hand. "How could you do this to me?" he shouted. "What are you? Some kind of freak who gets off on splitting married couples up or what?"

"Brad, please. It wasn't like that. I'm a woman now."

"Silence in court!" the judge called out, confused by the unfolding events.

"Have you fucking looked in the mirror lately? I've never seen a woman with a beard as full as that."

"Take the defendants down. Remove them both from my court," the judge said, repeatedly banging her gavel.

Miranda nudged the sniggering Caroline. "Look at the counsel. They look kind of sheepish, don't they?"

"I'm going to have a word with them before we leave, see what's going on."

The court remained silent as everyone listened to Brad screaming obscenities at Vanessa—or Luis—as they were both led back to their cells.

In the car, Caroline confided what the counsel had told her. "Apparently, Brad changed his counsel a few times and refused to listen to anything they said about Vanessa. He blamed her for making him kill Anneka and wanted nothing more to do with her. His solicitor tried to raise the subject about Vanessa being a transgender, but he refused to listen to anything concerning the woman. His arrogance in the end proved to be his downfall. Even his solicitor couldn't give a shit if he went to prison for life or not."

"Wow, seriously? It's not advisable to piss off the people fighting your corner, is it? What an idiot!"

Miranda smiled smugly at the thought of Anneka looking down, observing her husband's demise. *I bet she's laughing her socks off at this outcome.*

* * *

After finally being released from the confines of her mansion, Anneka sought out her grieving mother. When she'd overheard her parents talking about Vanessa and Brad's affair, everything had started to make sense at last. Anneka watched over her parents as they sat in the courtroom. She wanted to be there to see her cheating, murdering husband get what was coming to him. Nevertheless, she hadn't expected such an outcome. Her parents looked equally shocked.

When Brad lost his temper with his lover, Anneka looked over at the detective in charge of the case and joined in her laughter at Brad Lawrence's humiliation.

Realising that no one could hear her, she stood up, pointed at her husband, and shouted, "I will avenge my death, dear husband. I'll be around for eternity, forever watching you."

Note to the reader.

Thank you for reading Forever Watching You; I sincerely hope you enjoyed reading this novella as much as I loved writing it.

If you liked it, please consider posting a short review as genuine feedback is what makes all the lonely hours writers spend producing their work worthwhile.

ABOUT THE AUTHOR

New York Times, USA Today, Amazon Top 20 bestselling author, iBooks top 5 bestselling and #2 bestselling author on Barnes and Noble. I am a British author who moved to France in 2002, and that's when I turned my hobby into a career.
I share my home with two crazy dogs that like nothing better than to drag their masterful leader (that's me) around the village.
When I'm not pounding the keys of my computer keyboard I enjoy DIY, reading, gardening and painting.

Made in the USA
San Bernardino, CA
13 May 2016